THE

# ENGLISH AND AMERICAN
# SURREALIST POETRY

*English and American*

# SURREALIST POETRY

EDITED AND
WITH AN INTRODUCTION BY
*Edward B. Germain*

PENGUIN BOOKS

Penguin Books Ltd, Harmondsworth,
Middlesex, England
Penguin Books, 625 Madison Avenue,
New York, New York 10022, U.S.A.
Penguin Books Australia Ltd, Ringwood
Victoria, Australia
Penguin Books Canada Limited, 2801 John Street,
Markham, Ontario, Canada L3R 1B4
Penguin Books (N.Z.) Ltd, 182–190 Wairau Road,
Auckland 10, New Zealand

First published 1978
Reprinted 1979

Printed in the United States of America by
Kingsport Press, Inc., Kingsport, Tennessee
Set in Linotype Times Roman

# Contents

[Translations are listed by translator; brackets enclose the name of the author of the original poem.]

# CONTENTS

*Part II: The Second World War to the Present*

# CONTENTS

# CONTENTS

# Acknowledgements

For permission to reprint the poems in this anthology acknowledgement is made to the following:

For KENNETH ALLOTT: 'The Statue' from *Contemporary Poetry and Prose*, No. 4–5, August–September, 1936, to Miriam Allott.

For GEORGE ANTHONY: 'Autumn Evening' from *View*, IV, 1, March, 1944, to Charles Henri Ford.

For JOHN ASHBERY: 'Poem ("While we were walking under the top . . .")', 'Le Livre est sur la table' and 'Grand Abacus' from *Some Trees*, Yale University Press, 1956, to the author; 'They dream only of America' from *The Tennis Court Oath*, Wesleyan University Press, copyright © 1959 by John Ashbery, to the publisher.

For GEORGE BARKER: 'Calamiterror VI' from *Collected Poems 1930–55*, to the publisher, Faber and Faber Ltd. Originally published in *Calamiterror*, Faber and Faber, 1937.

For DJUNA BARNES: 'Transfiguration', originally published in *London Bulletin*, No. 3, June, 1938, revised version provided by the author, to the author.

For JOHN BAYLISS: 'Seven Dreams' from *View*, II, 3, October, 1942, and 'Apocalypse and Resurrection' published together with 'Seven Dreams' in *Indications*, Grey Walls Press, 1943, and in *The White Knight*, Fortune Press, 1944, to the author.

For JOHN BEEVERS: 'Atameros' from *Twentieth Century Verse*, No. 2, 1937, to Marjorie S. Beevers.

For TED BERRIGAN: 'Sonnet III', 'Sonnet LXX' from *The Sonnets*, Grove Press, 1967; 'Bean Spasms' from *Many Happy Returns*, Corinth Books, 1969, to the author; 'Orange Jews' to Ted Berrigan and Ron Padgett; excerpt from 'Memorial Day' from *Memorial Day: a collaboration*, The Poetry Project, 1971, to Anne Waldman and Ted Berrigan.

For ROBERT BLY: 'Waking from Sleep' and 'Snowfall in the Afternoon' from *Silence in the Snowy Fields*, Wesleyan University Press, 1962, to the author and publisher; 'At a March against the Vietnam War' and 'Counting Small-Boned Bodies' from *The Light Around the Body*, Harper and Row, 1968, to the author; 'An Extra Joyful Chorus for Those Who Have Read This Far' from *Sleepers Joining Hands*, Harper and Row, 1973, to the publisher. Translations by Robert Bly: Pablo Neruda's 'Walking Around', 'Nothing but Death' and 'Ode to the Watermelon'; César Vallejo's 'I have a terrible fear of being an animal', 'And don't bother telling me anything' and 'The anger that breaks a man down into boys' from *Neruda and Vallejo; Selected Poems*, edited by Robert Bly, Beacon Press, 1971, to Robert Bly; Tomas Tranströmer's 'Track', 'The Man Awakened by a Song Above His Roof', 'Allegro', 'Open and Closed Space' from *20 Poems of Tomas Tranströmer*, The Seventies Press, 1970, to Robert Bly. Translation by Robert Bly and James Wright: César Vallejo's 'Poem to be Read and Sung' from *Neruda and Vallejo; Selected Poems*, to Robert Bly.

For CHAINPOEMS: 'International Chainpoem', 'Lyric by Nine', 'Dirge for Three Trumpets' and 'Anglo-American Chainpoem' first published in *View*, reprinted in *New Directions*, No. 5, 1940, to Charles Henri Ford.

For TOM CLARK: 'You (I)' 'You (II)', 'You (III)', 'You (IV)', 'Daily News' and 'Superballs' from *Stones*, Harper and Row, 1969, to the author.

For ANDREI CODRESCU: 'poetry paper', 'a grammar' and 'work' from *The History of the Growth of Heaven*, Venture Books, George Braziller Inc., 1973; 'the imagination of necessity' from *A Serious Morning*, Capra, 1973, to the author.

For ROBERT CONQUEST: 'The Agents' from *Twentieth Century Verse*, No. 14, December, 1938, to the author.

For HARRY CROSBY: 'Firebrand', 'Vision' and 'Telephone Directory', to Harry T. Moore, literary executor of the estate of Caresse Crosby.

For HUGH SYKES DAVIES: 'Music in an Empty House' from *transition*, No. 18, November, 1929; 'Poem ("In the stump of the old tree ...")' from *Contemporary Poetry and Prose*, No. 7, November, 1936; 'Poem ("It doesn't look like a finger ...")' from *London Bulletin*, No. 2, May, 1938, to the author.

For TONI DEL RENZIO: 'Can You Change a Shilling?' from *View*, III, 3, October, 1943, to Charles Henri Ford.

For JOHN DIGBY: 'Sooner or Later' and 'One Night Away from Day', to the author.

For ROBERT DUNCAN: 'Eyesight II' from *Caesar's Gate*, to the author and publisher; *poems 1949–50*, Sand Dollar Press, 1950, to the author; 'Turning into' and 'Coming out of' from *Derivations; Selected Poems 1950–56*, Fulcrum Press, 1968, to the publisher.

For GAVIN EWART: 'Lifelines' and 'Lines' from *The Deceptive Grin of the Gravel Porters*, London Magazine Editions, 1968; 'Wanting Out' from *Pleasures of the Flesh*, Alan Ross Ltd, 1966, to the author.

For KENNETH FEARING: 'Evening Song' from *transition*, No. 2, May, 1927, to the author's literary estate.

ACKNOWLEDGEMENTS

For CHARLES HENRI FORD: 'Plaint' from *The Garden of Disorder and Other Poems*, New Directions, 1939; 'Somebody's Gone', 'January wraps up the wound of his arm', 'The Bad Habit' and 'The Overturned Lake' from *The Overturned Lake*, Little Man Press, 1941; 'There's No Place to Sleep in This Bed, Tanguy' from *Poems for Painters*, View Editions, 1945; all reprinted in *Flag of Ecstasy; Selected Poems*, Black Sparrow, 1972, to the author.

For DAVID GASCOYNE: 'The Very Image', 'The Cubical Domes', 'Salvador Dali', 'Yves Tanguy', 'The Truth is Blind' and 'The Cage' from *Collected Poems*, Oxford University Press, 1965, to the publisher; 'And the Seventh Dream is the Dream of Isis' and 'The End is Near the Beginning', originally published in *New Verse*, reprinted in *Man's Life is This Meat*, The Parton Press, 1936, to the Official Solicitor to the Supreme Court, acting on behalf of David Gascoyne. Translations by David Gascoyne: Hans Arp's 'The Domestic Stones (fragment)', André Breton's 'Postman Cheval' and 'The Spectral Attitudes', Salvador Dali's 'The Art of Picasso', Benjamin Péret's 'The Staircase with a Hundred Steps' and 'Making Feet and Hands', Pablo Picasso's 'Poems: "hasten on your childhood . . .", "in the corner a violet jug . . .", "in secret . . ."', Georges Ribemont-Dessaignes' 'Sliding Trombone', Pierre Unik's 'The Manless Society', all from *Collected Verse Translations of David Gascoyne*, edited by Robin Skelton and Alan Clodd, Oxford University Press, 1970, to the publishers.

For GEOFFREY GRIGSON: 'Before a Fall', from *New Verse*, No. 19, February–March, 1936, to the author.

For BERNARD GUTTERIDGE: 'Man into a Churchyard', from *New Verse*, No. 16, August–September, 1935, to the author.

For JOHN HAINES: 'Awakening', 'The Snowbound City', 'A Poem Like a Grenade', 'The Cloud Factory' and 'The Flight', copyright © 1966, 1967, 1968, 1968 by John Haines, from *The Stone Harp*, Wesleyan University Press, 1971, and Rapp and Whiting, 1971, to the author and publishers.

For DONALD HALL: 'Je suis une table' and 'The Alligator Bride' from *The Alligator Bride*, Curtis Brown Ltd, 1969, copyright © 1950, 1954, 1955, 1957, 1958, 1959, 1960, 1961, 1962, 1963, 1964, 1965, 1966, 1968, 1969 by Donald Hall, to the author and Curtis Brown Ltd; 'A Poet at Twenty' and 'Sudden Things', to the author.

For LEE HARWOOD: 'The Words' from *The Sinking Colony*, Fulcrum Press, 1970; 'Soft White', 'The "Utopia"' and 'The Final Painting' from *Landscapes*, Fulcrum Press, 1969, to the author.

For H. R. HAYS: 'The Sacred Children', 'January', 'The Case', 'Manhattan' and 'For One Who Died Young' from *Selected Poems*,

## ACKNOWLEDGEMENTS

Kayak Books, 1968, to the author.

For GEORGE HITCHCOCK: 'Song of Expectancy', published as a Unicorn Broadside, 1970; 'The One Whose Reproach I Cannot Evade' and 'The United States Prepare for the Permanent Revolution' from *The Dolphin with the Revolver in its Teeth*, Unicorn Press, 1967, to the author.

For ROBERT HORAN: 'By Hallucination Visited' from *View*, I, 9–10, December, 1941–January, 1942, to Charles Henri Ford.

For RANDALL JARRELL: 'The Islands' from *The Complete Poems of Randall Jarrell* reprinted by permission of Faber and Faber Ltd, and with the permission of Farrar, Straus and Giroux, Inc. from *The Complete Poems* by Randall Jarrell, copyright © 1965, 1966, 1967, 1968, 1969 by Mrs Randall Jarrell, to the publishers and Mrs Randall Jarrell.

For WELDON KEES: 'The Conversation in the Drawingroom' and 'The Heat in the Room' from *The Collected Poems of Weldon Kees*, copyright © 1960 by John A. Kees, reprinted by permission from the University of Nebraska Press, to the publisher.

For BILL KNOTT: '(End) of Summer (1966)', 'Sleep', 'Death', 'Hair Poem', 'Poem ("At your light side trees shy")', 'Poem ("After your death")', '(Poem) (Chicago) (The Were-Age)' and 'Goodbye' from *The Naomi Poems: Corpse and Beans*, Serendipity Press, 1968, to the author.

For KENNETH KOCH: 'You Were Wearing' from *Thank You and Other Poems*, Grove Press, 1962, to the publisher.

For SABUROH KURODA: 'Afternoon 3' from *View*, I, 6, June, 1941, to Charles Henri Ford.

For NORMAN MACCAIG: 'Poem ("There is a wailing baby under every stone . . .")' from *View*, I, 6, 1941; 'Betweens' from *Measures*, Chatto and Windus, 1965, to the author.

For CHARLES MADGE: 'Poem ("The walls of the maelstrom . . .")' from *London Bulletin*, No. 4–5, 1938; 'On One Condition', 'The Birds of Tin' and 'Landscape I' from *Poems*, Faber and Faber, 1937, to the author.

For ROBIN MAGOWAN: 'Zeimbekiko', 'Days of 1956', 'Susan' and 'Paros' from *Voyages*, Kayak Books, 1970, to the author.

For MICHAEL MCCLURE: 'Moiré', 'From the Window of the Beverly Wilshire Hotel' and 'May Morn' from *September Blackberries*, copyright © 1974 by Michael McClure, reprinted by permission of New Directions Publishing Corporation, to the publisher; 'Rant Block' from *The New Book/A Book of Torture*, Evergreen Books Ltd, 1961, to the author.

For THOMAS MCGREEVY: 'Homage to Hieronymus Bosch', originally published as 'Treasor of Saint Laurence O'Toole' in *transition*, No. 21, March, 1932, from *Collected Poems of Thomas McGreevy*, New Writers' Press, 1971, to Margaret Farrington and Elizabeth Ryan.

For GEORGE MELLY: 'Homage to René Magritte' from *Surrealist Transforma(c)tion*, No. 2, October, 1968, to the author.

For THOMAS MERTON: 'Lent in a Year of War' from *Selected Poems*, 1945, and *Collected Poems*, copyright 1946 by New Directions Publishing Corporation. Reprinted by permission of New Directions Publishing Corporation, New York.

For W. S. MERWIN: 'Bread', 'A Door', 'To the Hand', 'Glass' and 'The Diggers' from *Writing to an Unfinished Accompaniment*, Atheneum, 1973, to David Higham, London, the author's literary agent, and to the publisher.

For BERT MEYERS: 'Pigeons' from *The Dark Birds*, copyright © 1968 by Bert Meyers, reprinted by permission of Doubleday & Company, Inc., to the publishers; 'Suburban Dusk' and 'Daybreak', to the author.

For NIALL MONTGOMERY: 'Eyewash' from *Contemporary Poetry and Prose*, No. 8, December, 1936, to Curtis Brown Ltd, London.

For NICHOLAS MOORE: 'The Island and the Cattle', 'Song' and 'The Patient' from *The Island and the Cattle*, Fortune Press, 1941, to the author.

For PHILIP O'CONNOR: 'Poems 1–11' from *New Verse*, No. 24, February–March, 1937; 'Fag-End' from *Twentieth Century Verse*, No. 8, January–February, 1938; 'The Raspberry in the Pudding' from *Twentieth Century Verse*, No. 9, March, 1938, to the author.

For FRANK O'HARA: 'Poem ("The eager note on my door said 'Call me ...'")' and 'Blocks' from *Meditations in an Emergency*, Grove Press, Inc., copyright © 1957 by Frank O'Hara, reprinted by permission of Grove Press, Inc., to the publisher; 'Easter' from *The Collected Poems of Frank O'Hara*, edited by Donald Allen, copyright © 1969 by Maureen Granville-Smith, executrix of the Estate of Frank O'Hara, to the publisher, Alfred A. Knopf, Inc.

For RON PADGETT: 'After the Broken Arm' and 'December', originally published in *C Magazine*, and 'Strawberries in Mexico', originally published in *Angel Hair*, No. 5, all reprinted in *Great Balls of Fire*, copyright © 1965, 1967, 1968, 1969 by Ron Padgett, to the publisher, Holt, Rinehart and Winston, Inc.; 'Orange Jews' to Ted Berrigan and Ron Padgett.

For KENNETH PATCHEN: 'The Naked Land', 'In the footsteps of the walking air', 'A Temple' and 'Saturday Night in the Parthenon' from *Collected Poems*, copyright © 1942 by New Directions Publishing Corporation, copyright © 1943 by Kenneth Patchen, reprinted by permission of New Directions Publishing Corporation.

For ROLAND PENROSE: selections from *The Road is Wider Than Long: An Image Diary from the Balkans, July–August 1938*, London Gallery Editions, 1939, to the author.

For JOHN PERREAULT: 'Shoe' from *Camouflage*, Lines Press, 1966; 'Boomerang' from *Lines*, No. 2, December, 1964; 'Readymade' from *Nomad*, No. 8, Fall, 1960; 'The Metaphysical Paintings' from *Luck*, Kulchur Press, 1969, all to the author.

For JOHN CROWE RANSOM: 'Prelude to an Evening' in the version published in the *American Review*, April, 1934, and in *New Verse*, No. 10, August, 1934, rather than the revised version of 1963 in *Selected Poems*, Eyre & Spottiswoode, and in *Selected Poems*, Alfred A. Knopf, Inc./Random House, Inc., to Alfred A. Knopf/Random House, Inc.

For TOM RAWORTH: 'My Face Is My Own, I Thought', from *The Relation Ship* by Tom Raworth, Goliard Press, 1966; 'The Empty Pain-Killer Bottles,' 'Hot Day at the Races' and 'Collapsible' from *The Big Green Day* by Tom Raworth, Trigram Press Ltd, 1968, reprinted by permission of the author and the publishers.

For GEORGE REAVEY: 'Dismissing Progress and its Progenitors' from *Quixotic Perquisitions*, poems by George Reavey, Europa Press, 1939; 'How many fires' first read at the Surrealist Exhibition in London, 1936, published in *Frailties*, Blue Moon Press, 1975, to the author.

For EDOUARD RODITI: 'Seance', 'Hand' and 'Aurora Borealis' from *Prose Poems*, Kayak Books, 1968, to the author. Translation of André Breton's 'Freedom of Love' from *Young Cherry Trees Secured Against Hares*, University of Michigan Press, 1969, to the author.

For ROGER ROUGHTON: 'Soluble Noughts and Crosses; or, California, Here I Come' from *Contemporary Poetry and Prose*, No. 3, July, 1936; 'Building Society Blues' from *Contemporary Poetry and Prose*, No. 9, Spring, 1937, to Curtis Brown Ltd, London, on behalf of the Estate.

For SANDERS RUSSELL: 'Poem ("I keep feeling all space as my image . . .")' from *View*, II, 3, October, 1942, to Charles Henri Ford.

For FRANCIS SCARFE: 'The Merry Window' from *Contemporary Poetry and Prose*, No. 4–5, August–September, 1936; 'Ode in Honour' from *Contemporary Poetry and Prose*, No. 7, November, 1936; 'Kitchen Poem', to the author.

For HOWARD SERGEANT: 'Man Meeting Himself' from *New Road*, No. 5, 1949; 'The Inundation' from *Poetry Review*, London, both

ACKNOWLEDGEMENTS

published in *The Headlands*, Putnam and Company, 1953, to the author.

For A. J. M. SMITH: 'Political Intelligence' originally published as 'Political Note' in *Contemporary Poetry and Prose*, No. 7, November, 1936 to the author.

For KEN SMITH: 'Train' from *The Pity*, Jonathan Cape Ltd, 1968, to the publisher; 'Possessions', to the author.

For MARK STRAND: 'The Man in Black' and 'The Man in the Tree', originally published in *The New Yorker*, and 'The Marriage', originally published in *Partisan Review*, all from *Reasons for Moving*, copyright © 1966, 1967, 1968 by Mark Strand, reprinted by permission of Atheneum Publishers, U.S.A.; 'The Prediction' from *Darker*, copyright © 1970 by Mark Strand, reprinted by permission of Atheneum Publishers, U.S.A., to the publisher.

For JAMES TATE: 'Love Making' from *Notes of Woe*, Stone Wall Press, 1968; 'Dear Reader' from *Shepherds of the Mist*, Black Sparrow, 1969; 'The Pet Deer' and 'The Blue Booby' from *Row With Your Hair*, Kayak Books, 1969, to the author.

For DYLAN THOMAS: 'I, in My Intricate Image' and 'Because the pleasure-bird whistles' (originally titled 'January 1939'), both originally published in *Twentieth Century Verse*, No. 15–16, February, 1939, from the *Collected Poems of Dylan Thomas*, J. M. Dent & Sons, 1957, to the publisher and to the Trustees for the Copyrights of the late Dylan Thomas; also in *The Poems of Dylan Thomas*, copyright 1939 by New Directions Publishing Corporation. Reprinted by permission of New Directions Publishing Corporation, New York.

For RUTHVEN TODD: 'Paul Klee' from *London Bulletin*, No. 12, March, 1939; 'Poem ("I walk at dawn across the hollow hills ...")', 'Joan Miró (1937)' and 'Joan Miró (1947)' from *Garland for the Winter Solstice*, Atlantic-Little, Brown, 1961, to the author.

For HENRY TREECE: 'Horror' from *Invitation and Warning*, Faber and Faber Ltd, 1942; 'The Magic Wood' from *The Black Seasons*, Faber and Faber Ltd, 1945, reprinted by permission of the publisher.

For ANNE WALDMAN: excerpt from 'Memorial Day' from *Memorial Day: a collaboration*, The Poetry Project, 1971, to Anne Waldman and Ted Berrigan.

For YVOR WINTERS: 'The Precision' from *transition*, No. 7, October, 1927, to Janet Lewis Winters.

Every effort has been made to trace copyright holders, but in a few cases this has been impossible. The publishers would be interested to hear from any copyright holders not acknowledged.

To find the effects of surrealism on English language poetry, I read nearly every poetry magazine printed in English between 1920 and 1947. A few of these (*The London Bulletin, View, VVV*, for example) were edited by surrealists. Others printed special surrealist editions (*This Quarter, New Directions in Prose and Poetry, Contemporary Poetry and Prose*). Some (*transition, New Verse, Twentieth Century Verse*) sought out new experiments in poetry. Many did not. Nevertheless, I collected twelve hundred poems from which I assembled Part I of this book. Part II surveys surrealism in Anglo-American poetry after the Second World War.

Since the twenties, translations into English of surrealist poems from other languages often have served as an introduction to surrealism for Anglo-American poets. Space limitations preclude a survey of these translations, but I have included a few by three poets. David Gascoyne and Robert Bly are the two poets most responsible for translating a variety of surrealist poets into English. Edouard Roditi was André Breton's translator when Breton fled from Paris to New York at the beginning of the Second World War. Subsequently, he translated Breton's *Young Cherry Trees Secured Against Hares*, one of the first collections of Breton's poetry available in English.

The University of Michigan and Pomona College have provided research grants during various stages of this project. I would like to acknowledge the assistance of John Ashbery, Robert Bly, Robert Duncan, Donald Hall, Philip Lamantia,* Michael McClure and Edouard Roditi who, from their various points of view, have spoken with me about the focus and content of this book. I am grateful to those who took time to write about their work or that of others: Hugh Sykes Davies, Charles Henri Ford, Rod Padgett, John Perreault, George Reavey and Ruthven Todd. I am especially indebted to Donald Hall and J. H. Matthews for reading and commenting on the Introduction. Mary George at the Graduate

---

* I regret that copyright difficulties have prevented the inclusion of Philip Lamantia's poetry. His work belongs here. His recent collection is *Blood of the Air*, Four Seasons Foundation, 1970.

## Editor's Note

Library of the University of Michigan provided invaluable bio-graphical references. Sara Weeks Germain with her intelligence and visible beauty assisted this project at every stage.

# Introduction

## The Surrealist Tradition

The surrealist movement was founded in France in 1924, brother of the anarchist dada, heir to experiments in nineteenth-century literature too numerous to mention here and well documented elsewhere. It quickly became an international activity that grew symbiotically in the consciousness of artists. Wherever it arose, surrealism revealed itself as supra-literary, dedicated to the total recuperation of man's psychic forces from all aesthetic, moral, political and social constraints.

In England, it arose as the logical evolution of nineteenth-century literature's dominant concern: the psychopathology of the artist's mind. Being unconcerned with conventional morality, it had few affinities with the humanist tradition of literature and saw the classical tradition as antithetical to literature altogether. Herbert Read, member of the Surrealist Group in London, argues that the standards of classicism are intellectual concepts that repress growth and change, and that its values have always reflected the values of particular upper classes, intricately connected with class properties, class pleasure, class morality – not the 'standards of mankind', but Aristotle's standards or Sidney's standards, Addison's standards or Arnold's standards. The so-called 'universal truths of Classicism are the temporary prejudices of an epoch', Read concludes.

Both humanist and classicist mistake the poet's role, as Plato did when he excluded poets from his utopia because of their 'irrational character'. Surrealists admit that to a certain extent the poet *is* socially disruptive because his 'mental personality is originally determined by a failure in social adaptations'; nevertheless, 'his whole effort is directed towards a reconciliation with society'. Writing for the London Surrealist Group, Herbert Read:

In dialectical terms we claim that there is a continual state of opposition and interaction between the world of objective fact – the sensational and social world of active and economic existence – and the world of subjective fantasy. This opposition creates a state of disquietude, a lack of spiritual equilibrium, which it is the business of the artist to resolve. He resolves the contradictions by creating a synthesis, a work of art which combines elements from both these worlds, eliminates others, but which for the moment gives us a qualitatively new experience.

Dada had been anarchistic, burlesquing everything in and out of art that posed as truth but failed to offer a complete argumentation, eventually reducing the mental personality of the artist to its *ultima Thule*, a naïve state free from pretentiousness, habit, and arbitrary rules. Surrealism set out from this place to resolve the major discrepancies of life, to integrate the artist with society by integrating man with himself. The words that follow come from a 1936 position paper on British surrealism by Hugh Sykes Davies:

There are ... subtle and terrible ways in which the unconscious may ruin adult life. The unacted desires of our childhood, and the fears that went with them, can give rise to a continual undercurrent of anxiety in later years ... Sometimes the unconscious so far obtains the upper hand that it substitutes its own phantasies completely for normal reality ... To most of us there is [a] sign more impressive than any other of this world within us – the dream. Everyone knows how bad dreams can cast a shadow over the day that follows them, how they can destroy sleep. If you have ever walked in a city at night, you have heard the cry of the man, woman, or child who wakes in the midst of a nightmare on the brink of unthinkable crimes and sufferings ...

We are engaged in the exploration of the unconscious, in its conquest and final synthesis with the conscious – a synthesis by which the surreal will also become the surrational. We propose an extension of our control over territories hitherto uncontrolled – the kingdom of the irrational within ourselves ... The hidden world will become part of our common life as human beings, the anti-social will be made social, synthesized with the rest of our existence.

Art, whether painting, sculpture, or poem, gave the surrealists the way to locate and record aspects of the unconscious mind. Into their art went all their predispositions towards the unconscious, their interest in dreams, trance-states, hallucinations, delusions, paranoia – evocations of states of mind wherein processes apart from reason manifest themselves.

In this exploration, the English surrealists saw themselves descended from the tradition of the romantics. They looked back with interest to the dream literature of Coleridge's 'Ancient Mariner' and the hallucinatory clarity of 'Kubla Khan', to the mythopoeia of romanticism, to Keats's 'Fatal Woman', to Byron's 'Fatal Man', to the black or Gothic novels of Walpole, Ann Radcliffe, Charlotte Brontë, and the American, Charles Brockden Brown. They looked to Swinburne's intoxication with pleasure, to the fantasies of Edward Lear (called a better poet than Tennyson), and to Lewis Carroll. For Dryden and Pope they had only anger and pity, and before Scott, Dickens, or Hardy, they preferred Monk Lewis, Mrs Radcliffe, and Poe. They valued Shakespeare highly – Hamlet's struggle with madness takes on surrealist implications – and the irrational imagery of Milton.

They found the roots of surrealism within all poets who sought 'the kingdom of the irrational' within themselves: within Keats, whose 'negative capability' was to abnegate his ego and let the poem come almost automatically from forces seemingly beyond his control; within England's first poet, Caedmon, who after years of impotence burst into song when suddenly possessed by the holy spirit of God; within Hesiod, who, in the metaphor used by the Greeks, was possessed by the Muses (Hesiod notes that they instructed him how to sing praise of the future and the past); within the poet-priestess of the oracle at Delphi who became possessed by Apollo and uttered prophecies; within 'primitive' shamans, druids, priests – by whatever name the poet-as-vates is called in the archives of nearly every known culture; and finally within the deep structures of the mind itself, of which all these poems and prophecies are possessed.

'Nothing would be more erroneous', wrote Carl Jung in 1930,

than to assume that the poet creates rom the material of [literary] tradition. He works rather from primal experience ... The primal experience is word and imageless for it is a vision in the dark mirror ... That which appears in the vision is the collective unconscious, that curious structure inherited through the generations of the preliminary psychic conditions of the consciousness.

The important thing ... for ... literature lies in the fact that these manifestations of the collective unconscious have a compensatory character with relation to the state of [contemporary] consciousness; that is to say, that a one-sided, abnormal, dangerous state of consciousness is teleologically brought to equilibrium through it ... The work emerging from the collective unconscious is in the deepest sense of the word a message to contemporaries ... Every one of these poets, great or small, speaks with a voice of thousands and tens of thousands, predicting changes in the contemporaneous consciousness.

Jung's essay, published in *transition*, had enormous impact on English and American surrealists who recognized it as an ultimate argument against those rationalists who doubted the social value of surrealist poetry. Herbert Read:

What [the surrealist poet] offers to society is not a bagful of his own tricks, his idiosyncrasies, but rather some knowledge of the secrets to which he has had access, the secrets of the self which are buried in every man alike, but which only the sensibility of the artist can reveal to us ... largely made up of elements from the unconscious, and the more we learn about the unconscious, the more collective it appears to be.

Thus, it should be clear that in England as in France surrealism grew out of a frustration with rationalism, deeply conscious of the discoveries of Freud and Jung – the English group was more influenced by Jung, and sooner. Surrealism had reason to see itself as the crest of a tradition that sought the mysteries of the mind and which had always been the only *useful* tradition in poetry whether manifested mystically as vaticism, inefficiently as romanticism, or succinctly as surrealism. It sought the language of the unconscious.

## Automatism

Surrealism's basic technique was automatism, used by André Breton as early as 1919 when he and Philippe Soupault began writing the first automatic surrealist text, *The Magnetic Fields*. In the 1924 *Manifesto of Surrealism*, Breton recalls:

One evening ... before I fell asleep ... a rather strange phrase ... came to me ... something like 'There is a man cut in two by the window' ... accompanied ... by the faint visual image of a man cut half way up by a window perpendicular to the axis of his body. Beyond the slightest shadow of a doubt, what I saw was the simple reconstruction in space of a man leaning out a window. But this window having shifted with the man, I realized that I was dealing with an image of a fairly rare sort, and all I could think of was to incorporate it into my material for poetic construction. No sooner had I granted it this capacity than it was in fact succeeded by a whole series of phrases, with only brief pauses between them, which surprised me only slightly less and left me with the impression of their being so gratuitous ...

In a footnote to this passage, Breton speculates that were he a painter, the visual depiction would have become more important than the words, and he suggests that one way to evoke such images is starvation ('The fact is I did not eat every day during that period of my life'). Breton cites a passage from *Hunger* by Knut Hamsun, the Norwegian novelist who had won the Nobel Prize in literature four years earlier:

I wanted to go back to sleep, but I couldn't; ... a thousand thoughts were crowding through my mind ... All of a sudden I found, quite by chance, beautiful phrases, phrases such as I had never written ... And there were still more coming ... I picked up a pencil ... It was as though some vein had burst within me.

Both Breton and Hamsun remark that these surfacing phrases have about them a sense that they are absolutely right, even though, in Breton's words, they seem 'on the surface, as strange to you as they are to anyone else'. But upon closer scrutiny, they disclose 'properties and facts no less objective' than those in the external world. Such automatic phrases can become windows into the self, messages about the other side. I believe Breton's audible vision demonstrated this to him.

From the *First Manifesto*:

Secrets of the Magical
Surrealist Art
Written Surrealist Composition
or
First and Last Draft

After you have settled yourself in a place as comfortable as possible to the concentration of your mind upon itself, have writing materials brought to you. Put yourself in as passive, or receptive, a state of mind as you can. Forget about your genius, your talents, and the talents of everyone else. Keep reminding yourself that literature is one of the saddest roads that leads to everything. Write quickly, without any preconceived subject, fast enough so that you will not remember what you've written and be tempted to reread what you have written. The first sentence will come spontaneously, so compelling is the truth that with every passing second there is a sentence unknown to our consciousness which is only crying out to be heard. It is somewhat of a problem to form an opinion about the next sentence; it doubtless partakes both of our conscious activity and of the other, if one agrees that the fact of having written the first entails a minimum of perception. This should be of no importance to you, however; to a large extent, this is what is most interesting and intriguing about the surrealist game ... Go on as long as you like. Put your trust in the inexhaustible nature of the murmur.

Automatic writing uses the grammar of dreams, including language like this:

The woman with breasts of ermine was standing at the entrance of the passage Jouffroy in the light of songs ...
She was beyond our desires, like flames, and she was, as it were, the first day of the feminine season of flame, just one March 21st of snow and pearls.

Breton characterizes these automatic images as bringing together

two distant realities ... From the fortuitous juxtaposition of the two terms ... a particular light has sprung, the light of the image.

Freud has called this process 'condensation', when

dream-thoughts are ... turned into a collection of sensory images and visual scenes ... Such of them as have any point of [common] contact are condensed into new unities.

As the autonomously condensed image casts its light on a process of selection (dream-work) beyond rational control, 'the mind', Breton writes, 'becomes aware of the limitless expanses wherein its desires are made manifest'.

'Even more remarkable', Freud has written,

is the other process of *displacement* or transference of accent ... for the individual ideas which make up the dream-thoughts are not all of equal value. The importance of [repressed] ideas ... reappears in the dream in the form of the sensuous vividness of the dream pictures; but we notice that this accent, which should lie on important elements, has been transferred to unimportant ones.

Breton puts this in an aesthetic perspective:

Automatic writing ... is especially conducive to the production of the most beautiful images ... For me, their greatest virtue ... is the one that [appears] arbitrary to the highest degree, the one that takes the longest time to translate into practical language, either because it contains an immense amount of seeming contradiction or because one of its terms is strangely concealed ...

## The Real Functioning of Thought

No literary movement had ever understood so clearly the relationship between poetry and dreaming, or had so thoroughly blended poem and dream. Much of this insight was made possible by Freud, whose works Breton knew. But the hope in surrealism, the hope behind all surrealist activities, transcended anything Freud envisioned, affording to the dream an ontological reality ultimately superior to that of waking consciousness. 'Is it not possible', Breton asks in the 1924 *Manifesto*, 'that my dream of last night follows the one before, that dreams give every sign of being continuous?' Why should we not accord to the reality of dream the same status we give to the reality of daily life? Perhaps the dream can be a better counsellor than reason. Can it not offer a *superior intelligibility*, able to solve, as reason so obviously has not, 'the principal problems of life'?

Surrealism sought neither a romantic retreat into dreams nor a psychoanalytical reduction of dreams to the language of reason, but a dialectical synthesis of dream and reality, an equipoise:

The poet of the future will surmount the irreparable divorce of action and dream ... He will maintain at any price in each other's presence the two terms of the human relation ... the objective awareness of realities, and their internal development in ... the unconscious.

31

In this dialectical relationship, automatism is the window inward; its function is 'to reveal, verbally, by means of the written word, or in any other manner – the real functioning of thought'. But what is its 'real functioning'; what is it that surrealist poems, so baffling on the surface, mean? The answer is complex, and there are but few sources that treat the problem of interpretation this broadly. In this brief space, I should begin by insisting that it is absolutely necessary to take the poem *literally*. Critics who dismiss surrealism as senseless – meaning nothing – or as fantasy – meaning nothing real – fail at this initial step. If the poet writes 'A horse galloping on a tomato', that is *exactly* what he means, not that the horse trod on the tomato while passing by. Let me try to clarify this with an example.

## The Very Image

to René Magritte

An image of my grandmother
her head appearing upside-down upon a cloud
the cloud transfixed on the steeple
of a deserted railway-station
far away

An image of an aqueduct
with a dead crow hanging from the first arch
a modern-style chair from the second
a fir-tree lodged in the third
and the whole scene sprinkled with snow

An image of the piano-tuner
with a basket of prawns on his shoulder
and a fire-screen under his arm
his moustache made of clay-clotted twigs
and his cheeks daubed with wine

An image of an aeroplane
the propellor is rashers of bacon
the wings are of reinforced lard
the tail is made of paper-clips
the pilot is a wasp

An image of the painter
with his left hand in a bucket
and his right hand stroking a cat
as he lies in bed
with a stone beneath his head

And all these images
and many others
are arranged like waxworks
in model bird-cages
about six-inches high.

(David Gascoyne)

If I understand something of the normal reaction to this poem, the reader has found his mind moving through a helplessness of the reason. The process is incremental. Each stanza presents a tangible object that the next line confounds by a ludicrously inappropriate addition. The following lines force a further juxtaposition until the incongruity of contexts expands beyond reason's ability to encompass the meaning of the evolved image. Somewhere along this process the mind begins to turn back upon itself, observing the processes through which it has just gone, experiencing a perplexingly pleasant sense of the futility of the search for meaning.

One may become bewildered or even dizzy because of the distortions of scale – Gascoyne creates five tableaux of vast spaciousness (aqueducts, aeroplanes, churches in the distance) which suddenly telescope into six-inch-high bird-cages. And one may become disarrayed by the problem of reality: Gascoyne begins each stanza frankly with the words 'An image of . . .'. When the tableaux shrink, he carefully notes that the cages are *model* bird-cages, not the real thing. This may put the reader into the unsettling position of realizing that while there is nothing 'real' before him (it's just images), the images nevertheless exist. He finds them in the poem and in his mind. Something similar happens in René Magritte's painting of a smoker's pipe with the words beneath it announcing 'This is not a pipe.'

At any rate, faced with the irrefutable incongruities, the unexpected telescoping and astonishing vividness of the images in the poem, the reader may find his mind filled with a sense of wonder, or perhaps an irritating amusement which suggests the images are somehow significant, even though they are obviously products of mental activities with which normal consciousness is typically unfamiliar.

In his comments about the dream-process of condensation, Freud continues with these words:

... dream thoughts are condensed into new unities. When the thoughts are translated into pictures, those forms are indubitably preferred which allow this kind of telescoping, or condensation; it is as though a force were at work which subjected the material to a process of pressure or squeezing together.

Gascoyne's poem *embodies* this process.

Simultaneously with this recognition may come an awareness of the meaning latent in these images. In every stanza there is a movement towards a strange devitalization. His grandmother is decapitated, her head stuck upside-down on a spike, and abandoned. The aqueduct has a dead crow hanging from it enshrouded in snow. The piano-tuner turns into a mannikin. Even the aeroplane changes, into lard. The painter lies with his head on a stone in the posture of the dead. Some kind of sterility or fear hangs around this hilarious, entertaining poem.

The reader has found his rational faculties outstripped as the poem involves itself at a structural level with processes essentially unconscious in nature. To borrow a metaphor from scores of surrealist poems and paintings, the result is like the opening of doors in the mind. Or it *can be*. Reason is accessible, with its limits clearly felt. Unconscious desire, manifesting itself in the symbolic images, fills the conscious mind with wonder, or perhaps dread. Not clinging to either, perception watches the images surfacing, aware suddenly of the primal processes evolving effortlessly beneath it. Standing there, with all the doors open, is surreal.

This precise vantage point approximates that of the poet who opened similar doors to get his material, maintains equal access to both conscious and unconscious functionings of the mind, resolves their distances into an inter-communicating pattern to which the poem has been a map. The poem's full meaning is that state of mind, synchronistic, vividly aware of the images and the sound of their meeting, alert suddenly to a sense of the marvellous, feeling now that it will never end.

## The Crisis of Automatism in England

Automatism is one surrealist technique, one touchstone. Until about 1927 or 1928 it dominated the movement, but eventually automatic images became monotonous, fell into predictable patterns. Critics were swift to expose surrealist 'formulas' such as 'the — of the —': 'the craters of his eyes', 'the threads of her heart', 'the snakes of her hair', 'the lids of her windows', 'the houses of their blood', 'the key-hole of your eye', 'her thoughts of heat-lightning'.

In response, the surrealists accused the critics of refusing to look deeply into surrealism, thereby misconstruing its experiences as fantastic idylls. There was also truth in this counter-charge. The war concerned language in a primary sense. Critics perpetuated the language of reason, assuring their public, at least by implication, that its habituated, common-sense pattern of the world was sufficient and reasonably accurate. The surrealists, on the other hand, knew that the unconscious always works beneath the daily perceptions of common-sense. Freud had theorized this. The problem was to catch it in the act in such a way that the experience could be communicated to others.

In 1928, Salvador Dali formulated his paranoiac-critical technique which, though revolutionary, turns out to be as old as the surrealist impulse. Leonardo da Vinci describes an early version of it in his notebooks when he speaks about seeing faces and landscapes in a cracked wall. To a degree, Shakespeare presents the phenomenon in *Hamlet*:

HAMLET: Do you see yonder cloud that's almost in the shape of a camel?

POLONIUS: By the mass, and 'tis like a camel indeed.

HAMLET: Me thinks it is like a weasel.

POLONIUS: It is backed like a weasel.

HAMLET: Or like a whale?

POLONIUS: Very like a whale.

Traditional critics say this passage shows Hamlet trying to humiliate Polonius by showing him to be a sycophant. He fails because Polonius obtusely thinks Hamlet mad and so merely humours him. The surrealist critic looks beneath the dialogue for its underlying structure of thought; he finds critical-paranoia.

'Paranoia', wrote Dali, 'uses the external world in order to assert its ... idea, and has the disturbing characteristic of making others accept this idea's reality.' Paranoia does not obliterate reality, nor surrender to subjectivism. The mammals in the clouds depend as much upon cloud-shapes as upon Hamlet's inner desire to transform them. For the surrealists the remarkable thing is that Polonius can witness the transformation.

In painting, Dali produced double-images where without physical change one object simultaneously represents another. In poetry, the technique becomes a *demonstrable* way of turning one image into another without resorting to metaphor (a snow-covered barn into a ship, sodden leaves into ancient letters). Hugh Sykes Davies's 'Poem' on page 104 presents a kaleidoscopic series of such transformations that also makes the distinction between critical-paranoia and the mental disease. It begins a little like the conversation between Hamlet and Polonius:

It doesn't look like a finger it looks like a feather of broken glass

but differs by not identifying the object under paranoiac scrutiny. It quickly becomes clear, however, that the subject is a great man-made destruction which has left many dead and reduced buildings to rubble; women survive it, but it has made them old. It is recognizably war.

A variety of internal evidences, together with the date of the poem (one year after the Barcelona uprising), reveals the war to be the take-over of Spain by the fascists, who are portrayed as psychopathic. Their minds, filled with paranoid delusions, decay like 'rotten fruit' in a bowl. They manifest their sickness by aggression and atrocities. Davies leads them from one transformation to another ('it doesn't look like a feather it looks like a finger with broken wings'), to reveal the psychotic repressions that surface as their brutal, sadistic relationships – the tyranny of the unconscious over critical intelligence. The last few lines make of the poem a curse, condemning the fascists to the hell of their own making, where anything they see will be used against them by their unconscious, where all their vicious acts will be forever held against them by free men.

Critical-paranoia in contrast, the poet's ability to transform objects with a detached awareness, forms a supremely healthy, vigorous force which enables him to confute the fascists again and again ('it doesn't look like a finger it looks like a feather with broken teeth').

The reader experiences both what the fascist sees and what Davies knows; both the shape of psychotic delusions and the vigorous reshaping of that deluded world by the power of the poet's integrated mind. In general terms, he sees a way the mind works, and a way it misfunctions. If he is a good reader, he becomes freed from his own pre-learned, common-sense representations of the world long enough to recognize that along perceptual pathways an object can exist in many forms – he has just experienced some of these in his own mind. If he is free enough, he may then see how every object of his *own* world is not what it appears, and how it is. And if he perceives this, he begins to remove the antinomies between reality and dream, between fact and desire. Breton:

Surrealism, such as I conceive of it, asserts our complete *non-conformism* clearly enough . . . This world is only very relatively in tune with thought . . . Surrealism is the 'invisible ray' which will one day enable us to win out over our opponents. This summer the roses are blue; the wood is of glass. The earth draped in its verdant cloak makes as little impression upon me as a ghost.

The paranoiac-critical technique was one solution to the formulaic monotony and the merely neurotic ('Freudian') contents of the images produced by automatism. Gradually it became clear to the French surrealists that they had deceived themselves by believing in the self-sufficiency of automatic 'thought' – which was, after all, only half the story. In 1934, Breton announced that surrealism must 'cease being content with . . . automatic texts, the recital of dreams, improvising speeches, spontaneous poems, drawings and actions'. *What Is Surrealism?*, which David Gascoyne translated in 1936, goes on to explain that surrealism will henceforth consider these 'as being simply so much material' to use in its search for a unified expression of the continuity between events in the conscious and unconscious worlds.

Yet the public had for so long identified surrealism with automatism that it would not really *see* the new emphasis. As the Second World War approached, this lack of vision created for surrealism a crisis of belief that was nowhere more severe than in England.

## The Surrealist Group in England

The first call for surrealism in England had come, surprisingly enough, from Oxford University, in 1927. A nineteen-year-old student from France, Edouard Roditi, wrote an essay, 'The New Reality', about the problem of becoming a poet in the face of the accomplishments of Eliot, Stein, Joyce, Cummings, Pound and other 'established' writers. He finds that one attitude common to them all is *precision*, an obsession with 'exactly where to place each word'. To be more than just an imitator, he reasons, the young poet can challenge this dominant attitude. It is possible to revolt against it 'by bringing an element of chance into poetry. This element of chance is Surrealism.'

At the time, few seem to have noticed this enthusiastic essay in the conservative *Oxford Outlook*. Five years passed before anyone again attempted to introduce surrealism to an English audience, and it was not until about 1935 that surrealism in England became much more than an idea. That year David Gascoyne published *A Short Survey of Surrealism*, which related the movement to its vatic forbears and established it as the heir of nineteenth-century English Romanticism. That year Gascoyne also wrote the only English manifesto of surrealism, in French ironically, which preceded by a few months the founding of the Surrealist Group in London.

The Group's platform was orthodox surrealism: anti-Government, anti-Church, anti-Art, post-Freudian in advocating the supremacy of the pleasure principle and the transformation of life by desire. Members of the group were enormously energetic. They

published, painted, sculpted, and organized a fantastically success-
ful International Exhibition of Surrealism in June 1936, which, in
the words of the *Bystander*, 'set more tongues wagging in passion-
ate disagreement than any exhibition since the Post-Impressionists
first bewildered London'.

Breton opened the exhibition; attendance averaged nearly 1,500
a day. There were lectures and readings by Breton, Herbert Read,
Paul Éluard, Davies, Dali, Gascoyne, Humphrey Jennings, George
Reavey. While one lecture was going on constantly interrupted
by the ringing of a bell, Dylan Thomas walked through the rooms
offering boiled string in teacups and politely asking, 'Weak or
strong?' The exhibition, which included work by artists from
nineteen countries, including Japan, drew more people than any
London art show ever had, and 'marked the highest point in the
graph of the influence of our movement', according to Breton.

However, the surrealists in England soon began to experience
the frustration of making social and political comments in a medium
that the public, for all its curiosity, regarded as a freak-show. With
the fall of Spain and the incremental advance of the Nazis through
Europe, it seemed more and more essential to be understood. But
even the Marxists, who should have been the surrealists' natural
allies, found their behaviour bewildering. Finally, Gascoyne
defected, commenting:

The French Surrealists themselves have a definite justification for
writing in this way, but for an English poet with continually growing
political convictions it must soon become impossible.

The Surrealist Group in London continued a formal existence
at least until 1947. But only one member of the original group,
Roland Penrose, remained in it to sign its final statement of dis-
solution. All these artists dropped away during the war: Eileen
Agar, Edward Burra, Hugh Sykes Davies, Mervyn Evans, David
Gascoyne, Charles Howard, Humphrey Jennings, Rupert Lee,
Sheila Legge, Len Lyn, Henry Moore, Paul Nash, Man Ray,
Herbert Read, George Reavey, Roger Roughton, Ruthven Todd,
Julian Trevelyan.

## The New Apocalypse

During this period of waning, one group deserves brief mention. A half-dozen writers immodestly calling themselves 'The New Apocalypse' revolted against what they mistakenly imagined to be 'Surrealism's own denial of man's right to exercise conscious control ... of his political and social destinies ... or of the material offered to him as an artist by his subconscious mind'.

Henry Treece, Nicholas Moore, John Bayliss, George Barker, J. F. Hendry (the latter not included in this anthology) and, for a time, Dylan Thomas, wrote poems that created dream-like states through symbolism, fairy-tale and myth. But instead of juxtaposing diverse realities, the Apocalyptic poet desired 'to combine, to fuse into a justifiable whole, his several sets of experience'. This was, of course, a new romanticism, Art unconcerned with revelation, showing little faith in the powers of the irrational. Compared with Breton's

I am growing old and, more than that reality to which I believe I subject myself, it is perhaps the dream, the difference with which I treat the dream, which makes me grow old ...

how pessimistic Moore is:

... all their dreams were hopeless with the worm.

To these romantics, the convulsive beauty of surrealism appeared destructive; the more beautiful it seemed, the more demonic it surely was. They wondered with Kathleen Raine:

Had such [surrealist] art been, after all, cathartic, or had it played its part in the loosing of the devils into a possessed world.

Breton, of course, looked at it differently; he blamed the system of world views that precipitated and prosecuted the war:

very well then, system ... Mind what you're about ... If this war and the many chances that it offers you to live up to your promise were to be in vain, I should be forced to admit that there is something a bit presumptuous about you, or for all anybody knows, something basically wrong with you that I can no longer hide from myself. In like manner poor mortals once prided themselves on having put the devil in his place, which made him decide, they say, to finally show himself in person.

## Surrealism in America

The first important exhibition of surrealist paintings outside France was held in Hartford, Connecticut, in 1931. Another quickly followed in New York at the Julian Levy Gallery. In December 1936, the Museum of Modern Art held its spectacular exhibition *Fantastic Art, Dada, and Surrealism*. From then on, surrealist art was exhibited almost continuously in New York through the Second World War.

Not all the exhibits were in museums. In 1939, Salvador Dali created a display in the windows of Bonwit Teller, crashing through the plate-glass while struggling to position a fur-lined bathtub. At the World's Fair held in New York that year, a surrealist exhibit showed 'liquid ladies' floating through water with an undulating piano, an exploding giraffe, botanical typewriters, occasionally milking a cow – all against the background of ruined Pompeii, while Venus lay on a couch thirty-six feet long 'dreaming the dreams of all mankind'.

While these surrealist exhibitions are landmarks, American art and literature had shown earlier affinities with the spirit of surrealism that most literary historians overlooked. It is difficult to document this relationship in such a brief space, but I can sketch a few highlights.

In the first place, surrealism had grown up with dada, and dada was born in New York in 1913. It was also born more or less simultaneously in several European countries, but not in England. Its nihilistic and witty assaults on convention, its happenings and outrageous public provocations, were closer to the American spirit. One cannot conceive, for example, of Picabia's entry in the 1913 Armory Show being hung in a prominent London gallery: a framed dead monkey surrounded by the words 'Portrait of Rembrandt, Portrait of Cézanne, Portrait of Van Gogh: Still Life.'

While dada was growing up in America, so were moving pictures, and like dada they were primarily an American, rather than a British, phenomenon. Dada had introduced into art the new experience: doubt. Silent films introduced motion, the essence of which was desire. Thwarted or rewarded, desire moved the plot, cast the waif into the snow, rescued the heroine from the wheels of the train, sent the car careening madcap down Fifth Avenue. Buster Keaton, Charlie Chaplin, Laurel, Hardy, the Marx Brothers and others moved with ease through a reality so expanded by imagination, so filled with unexpectedly juxtaposed events, that it approached the surreal. I think of Buster Keaton being chased by hundreds of women, each wanting to be his wife. He dashes down a hillside suddenly to find himself in the middle of a ponderous avalanche of huge boulders. Is this not conscious dream?

Silent films fascinated Breton and his friends. They tried running from one cinema to the next, attending several in one night, entering and leaving at random times, thus effectively splicing together in their minds their own film. 'My friends,' announced Aragon, 'opium, the shameful vices, and the alcoholic symphony are all out of style: we have invented movies.'

The films they actually made were significant failures. Man Ray's *Étoile de mer* (1928), Luis Buñuel and Salvador Dali's *Un Chien andalou* (1929) and *L'Âge d'or* (1930) all seem contrived and self-conscious compared to the best of Hollywood's silent comedies. Nevertheless, it is easy to see that what attracted them to film is the same thing that packed Americans into theatres: its simulation of a world where dream and reality visibly interpenetrate.

In other words, certain developments on the frontiers of American art had surrealist proclivities. Film is a good example of this, another is the experimental poetry of Samuel Greenberg and William Carlos Williams. Greenberg began mixing dream and reality to create new moods in poetry before dada was born. *Kora in Hell* (1920) finds Williams mindful of the innovations of the Armory Show, which he mentions in his preface to the second edition. In *Kora* he combines prose and poetry, fantasy and analysis, and blends Greek myth into modern life to create a world of transformations that can follow the shifting course of his own mind and desires. *Kora* is full of proto-surrealist imagery:

This is what they found in the rock when it was cracked open: this fingernail.

and

The ears are water. The feet listen.

After the publication of Breton's *First Manifesto*, Williams began to insist upon the role of automatism in creativity ('Only one answer; write carelessly so that nothing that is not green will survive'). He also agreed with the surrealists that the purpose of art is to put the powers of the unconscious at the disposal of the waking mind. When Jung's article appeared in *transition* in 1930, Williams exulted:

We've heard enough of the cant that the artist is a born weakling, that his works are effects of a neurosis, sublimations, escapes from the brutal contact with life that he, poor chap, horribly fears. This has always been said, and Freud seemed to put the last nail in the coffin with his discoveries. But, as reported in the last number of *transition*, an abler man than Freud, Dr C. G. Jung, has finally revealed the true state of affairs to be profoundly in favor of the poet. It is he, the poet, whose function it is, when the race has gone astray, to lead it – to destruction perhaps, but in any case, to lead it.

One could trace the actual contacts Williams had with surrealists,* or extricate the surrealist threads in *Kora* or in his intricate poem *Paterson* – especially those which correspond with Breton's 'Prolegomena on a Third Manifesto ...' of 1942. Taken as a whole, his work falls short of surrealism on its romantic side. But taken one poem at a time, it reflects an American handling of essentially surrealist themes: the impulse to awake the citizenry who were 'locked and forgot in their desires ... unroused'; the need to connect daily life with deep mythic roots; the desire to revolutionize consciousness. But with Williams these matters remained goals within art, for he believed in art, and did not share

*Williams wrote introductions to the first two surrealist-oriented magazines published in America, *Blues* and *View*, and another introduction to the first book of American surrealist poems, Charles Henri Ford's *Garden of Disorder* (1938). Breton, Nicholas Calas and Robert Motherwell asked him to be on the editorial board of the surrealist extravaganza *VVV*, published in New York, 1942–4. Williams declined, and the advisory board became Breton, Duchamp and Ernst, but he subsequently contributed to the magazine.

the ambivalence of the European surrealists towards it. Like other American poets and artists, he could also believe in the essential innocence of daily America and in its potential to solve the 'principal problems of life'. Poetry could be a means of awakening perception, he thought, that would reveal deep layers of self. In this he joined the European surrealists. But he lacked their direct and shattering experience of a World War at home – experience that, redirected as dada, destroyed all boundaries and limitations of art and gave to surrealism its obsessive moral urgency. As a result, in Williams's work and in American art in general until the Second World War, surrealism remains latent within romanticism and fantasy.

The exception to this was Charles Henri Ford, who was for the entire decade of the thirties America's sole dedicated surrealist poet. In 1940, when he founded the surrealist magazine *View*, Edith Sitwell called him the leader of the surrealist group in New York. But that was a series of loose affiliations, neither as organized nor as focused as the London Group. It had no manifesto, and included three men: Ford, the painter Tchelitchew, and Parker Tyler, America's first surrealist critic of films.

Ford's own poetry is authentic American surrealism – it doesn't sound like a translation from the French – American in its eclecticism, its hilarity and ingenuousness and fascination with sex and slang and the lyrics of popular songs. His poetry is full of kinky jazz blues:

> I must say your deportment took a hunk
> out of my peach of a heart.
> I ain't insured against torpedoes!
> My turpentine tears would fill a drugstore

and witty satires of popular lyrics:

> And the lasso of love has the ghost of a chance ...

His forte is the lyrical surrealist image. He can write astonishing first lines:

> I believe in the day hung between your hands,

breathtaking endings:

> leaving the body desolate as a staircase.

In between, he creates miraculous images. The reader will find them.

## Surrealism as International Modernism

The war radically changed the situation of surrealism in America. It brought many intellectuals and artists to New York, including Breton, Dali, Ernst, Tanguy, Duchamp, Seligmann and others involved in European surrealism. Their exhibitions, lectures at colleges and universities, and the friendships they formed that would otherwise not have occurred, gave the development of American surrealism an enormous momentum.

When the war began, Americans, poets among them, still believed it could be won. Shortly, as the depravities of the war were exposed, this illusion evaporated. Concentration camps, gas chambers, the Nüremburg trials, atomic bombs, radioactive fallout, ended the age of American isolation and innocence. America's essentially puritanical naïveté was torn open. Suddenly romanticism and fantasy, so strong a few years earlier, seemed escapist diversions, and the need that had for twenty years dominated surrealism in Europe became an American need, to find an incorruptible base for hope, for new shapes of perception, new actions, new language: a new reality. Suddenly the old reality was filled with devils and death.

At this time, surrealism appeared as the only aesthetic able to integrate the vast shiftings going on everywhere. It had in fact foreshadowed many of them. As early as 1924, for example, it had been clear that the surrealists were the first post-Freudians in art, recognizing the potential supremacy of the pleasure principle over the reality principle and simultaneously calling for a new morality drawn in accord with desire:

the magnificent discoveries of Freud reveal to us [that] the nature of human relationships threatens to destroy even those institutions hitherto considered as the most reliable ... and, after the ruin of a derisive moral code, awakens the expectation of a veritable science of morality.

Their even more basic attitude, their 'refusal to belong to any school of thought, the repudiation of the adequacy of any body of beliefs whatever, and especially of systems, and a marked dissatisfaction with traditional philosophy as superficial, academic, and removed from life', made surrealism a parent of existentialism, the tremulous philosophy evolving from the war years. Indeed, the passage just cited which describes surrealism so aptly comes from the introduction to Kaufman's *Existentialism*, and was meant to delineate the basic tenets of that movement.

In 1936, Breton traced for the first time in English the common parameters of surrealism and the new sciences, concluding:

> I have endeavoured to show how the *open rationalism* which defines the present position of scholars (as a sequel to the conception of non-Euclidean ... geometry, non-Newtonian mechanics, non-Maxwellian physics, etc.) cannot fail to correspond with the *open realism* or *Surrealism* which involves the ruin of the edifice of Descartes and Kant and seriously disturbs sensibility.

In a graduate seminar on surrealism, Herbert Marcuse asked his students (in an exam) whether surrealism had anything to do with the Paris student uprisings in 1968. While the net of interconnections is elaborate, the answer is 'yes' – just as surrealist attitudes influenced the Beat and subsequently the Hippie movement in America, while rock music groups named themselves in surrealist images (Led Zeppelin etc.). When the Museum of Modern Art in New York held a Dada and surrealism retrospective in 1968, the opening was picketed by politically radical 'Yippies' who claimed that *they* were the living surrealists. Inside the museum, Salvador Dali reportedly agreed, adding with an uncharacteristic sigh, 'but we were always aristocrats'.

When the war ended, most European artists left New York, but surrealism remained, the only revolutionary movement in poetry. In the next decade it spread across America, and also resurfaced in England. The extension of its influence is visible in this anthology.

At present orthodox surrealist groups exist in both countries. The English group publishes a vigorous little magazine, *Surrealist Transforma(c)tion*; the work of the group in Chicago can be seen in the 1974 *City Lights Anthology*. But the time seems to have passed when surrealist *organizations* can be very effective. Since the war, surrealist groups in over two dozen countries have dwindled or dissolved. New or reformed groups often seem embarrassing repetitions. Surrealism itself survives, but not as dogma; it survives as a strategy of mind. It is the only aesthetic to attack principal questions and to offer an integrity that combines psychological, political, philosophical, practical and aesthetic implications.

Unfortunately or not, it has also survived piecemeal in popular music, on billboards, in advertisements (there were surrealist-influenced posters in the London subways in the early thirties), and as an influence upon myriad revolutionary political groups. Often, in these contexts, it remains poorly understood, as this outrageously satirical letter, written by John Ashbery to Yippie leader Jerry Rubin ten years ago in *Art News*, suggests:

Mr Rubin ought to remember that not only is he a surrealist but that Alfred Barr and the trustees of the Museum of Modern Art are too; that all artists now working in America (except Frank Stella and Kenneth Noland, for reasons I cannot fathom) are surrealists; that Thomas B. Hess, Clement Greenberg and Hilton Kramer are surrealists; that President Johnson is a surrealist; that Congress is 95 percent surrealist and that the entire nation and the world including Vietnam are surrealist places.

A footnote: from the *Congressional Record*, 16 August 1949:

All these isms are of foreign origin, and truly should have no place in American art. While not all are media of social or political protest, all are instruments and weapons of destruction ... Surrealism aims to destroy by the denial of reason ... The evidence of evil design is everywhere ... The question is, what have we, the plain American people, done to deserve this sore affliction that has been visited upon us so direly; who has brought down this curse upon us; who has let into our homeland this horde of germ-carrying art vermin?

Congressman George A. Dondero
(reprinted in *Arsenal: surrealist subversion*)

## The Poems

Let us look at the central problem for the modern poet who sees through the posturings of that hanger-on, convention, and looks at so-called 'civilized life' with clean eyes. Why write? Why write when he can sell insurance and appear to all the world as indispensable? Of what weight is a poet set against the legislator, prime minister, or cabinet official? This year street-sweepers in San Francisco earn $17,000 and promote health besides. But the poet, perched above North Beach, sheltered or exposed to the sun, unpaid, brooding soul . . . what *good* is it that he writes? On what justification can his images rest? What defence can still be erected against even the garbage-collector's charge of self-indulgence, fantasy, and irrelevant dreaming, things Americans no longer tolerate very well.

Rats are interesting because we fear them. Insurance measures our concern with death. Legislators, all of them, work not only from beneficent desires for others (and themselves), but equally from fear of what would happen if the laws came down, if the asylums split open, and each man could take what he dared.

The poet who hears surrealism knows three worlds: the world of objects (rats and brooms and garbage), the world of abstract ideas (insurance policies and laws), and the world of desire, unconscious desire that *recognizes* events in the other two. *What* we desire surfaces through the unknowable maze of the subconscious to reappear with hallucinatory fascination as money or lovers, forgettings or rememberings, objects and ideas that seem to present a complete reality, but which are merely shadows cast far.

The surrealist poet's concern is this shadow-casting activity which he investigates on its proper ground, not in the weakening daylight of 'reality' that erases subtle colorations and the most delicate shapes, but on the scrim of the mind where in each case two different sets of shadows appear. One is cast by the object or idea as seen. This is always a distortion, though the distorting activity in perception does not necessarily imply anything about the object or idea itself – especially about its 'real' or ideal existence. Perception is character. We walk among shadows of ourselves.

The second set is cast upon the eye of the mind from within. The images of dreams, of automatism, are of this sort. Who can say if they are distorted; they are indisputably written in the grammar and language of thought. They, too, are evidences of 'character', but not that hammered out by societal and parental smiths.

'Of what good are these sets of images?' society asks.

They are simply all we have.

The poet asks the legislator if the law is a good one. Unless the legislator can see its relationship to innermost desires, how can he answer?

'What good is the broom?' the poet asks the street-cleaner, who is apt to start sweeping in reply or to hold up his salary for the poet to see. All the while the broom waves its hair to the poet and shivers its cylindrical flesh at the puerility to which imagination can descend.

As for the justification of his images, the poet knows without fear or qualification that they are real. What he seeks is the single pattern of which they are parts.

Breton closed the *First Manifesto* with this thought:

It is living and ceasing to live that are imaginary solutions. Existence is elsewhere.

*

The poet asks the legislator if the war is a good one – Robert Bly's 'At a March against the Vietnam War'. The legislator leaks darkness that fires up like a stream of gunpowder. It burns towards the secretaries in the hall, towards the protest marchers on the field, towards the poet. It is a fire of fear oozing from us all. We call it 'national policy'. It is a cry. Howard Sergeant heard it in England. It survived the Second World War. 'And the cry is guilt – man meeting himself in the night.'

He is a 'Queer Thing', Emanuel Carnevali saw after the First World War, who hates his head because it will 'not fall of itself like any decent pear. It has the intention of flying up to the sky', but it eats 'grime and dirt', screams 'erotic songs', and buries itself in one or another half of the schizophrenia engendered by

Puritanism. We make war against our own shadow. The poet stands watching, implicated almost beyond redemption. Impotently, John Haines hopes for poems that become grenades 'casually dropped into a basket among the desks of the wrongheaded statesmen'.

It is no mere coincidence that the revolutionary Students for a Democratic Society gave the guest editorship of their magazine, *Radical America*, to the Surrealist Group in Chicago at about the same time that an outwardly conventional poet represented in this anthology gave aid to people who had blown up selective service files, hiding them from the F.B.I. There are common denominators between John Haines's investigations of the dream-like atmosphere of *inevitable disaster* rising from our civilization during the late sixties and André Breton's investigations of the erotic dreams French women had of German officers just before France fell.

Psychosis masquerading as civilization forms the subject of so many poems, Hays's 'The Case', for instance, or Perreault's 'Readymade', or Clark's 'Superballs', O'Hara's 'Easter' ... it would take a page to list them all. The poet's view of the insanely regimented obsessions of civilization often take the form of black humour — Péret, Roughton, or Harry Crosby's 'Telephone Directory'. There is a poem, not included here, in which Charles Henri Ford starts to rename a hundred hotels in New York and Paris, letting his free associations build up connotations of their own. They become so full of foreboding that he gives up in despair.

Robert Bly writes poem after poem showing how U.S. foreign policy in Vietnam, in South America, is the result of our fears and the weaknesses of our leaders. David Gascoyne throws his tobacconist down the stairs like a Christian and Frank O'Hara kills his host with kindness, but they were too busy listening to the message from the agent of fear to notice. He's up there now, Robert Conquest sees him, with 'his head like a fist rooted in his abdomen' sailing little tin birds down this way. Charles Madge catches one, but its municipal wings won't open. Niall Montgomery watches the agent 'clock out important messages on his vanishing brain', and then steps away to wash out his eyes. The rest of us stand there as though our eyes were onions.

Beaten down, deafened, ignored, Robert Bly walks away from a poetry reading in California screaming 'When you go out of here, reality's not going to be what you think it is!'

\*

Reality, the changed reality of the twentieth century ... The physicist begins to explain reality as particle flow within a field of probability. Though he talks about physics, we recognize a flowing, transforming world expressed in these poems with a boldness not found in nineteenth-century poetry when this world-view was in embryo, nor in poetry written after the traditions of that century. In 1941, Charles Henri Ford changes the day from a free autonomous poem into a horse. He turns the sky into an arm, a mouth, a man, a thief, and then into an enormous face. The sun he makes into a wound, a jewel, an equation, an eye, a tear. Night is a ditch. All in eight lines, with obvious ease, clarity and probable cause; flowing particles of desire condense and are displaced again, by others.

Reality, says the scientist, is entropic and may seek higher forms of probability – where probability means we can't know for sure. Is this the 'Daily News' Tom Clark unravels from the life of a child who carries a grey torch into the future when he hurls his first toy? Or perhaps it is the untransformed *ground* of wind that Bravig Imbs feels as he dies, and that Mark Strand sees we are married to. 'The wind is strong, he thinks as he straightens his tie.'

We see a Baudelairean relationship between science, poetry and nature introduced by Charles Madge in 'Landscape I', and a more sophisticated evolution by Michael McClure in 'Moiré', a synthesis of paleontology, Buddhism, astronomy, poetry, mythological archetypes, dreams, ecology, botany, and molecular biology, dedicated to Francis Crick, the co-discoverer of the double-helix structure of the DNA molecule.

'Moiré' confronts the duality-ridden western world-view of unlimited growth and expansion ('progress') with a unified vision of man in a symbiotic relationship with a stabilized environment. McClure finds as far back as the late paleolithic evidence of man's evolving psyche that supports such a view.

Nearly every poem in this anthology assumes modern concepts

of space/time: as a relativistic continuum in Lee Harwood's 'The Words', where the linear time of syntax breaks into spatial pauses full of unarticulated meanings, as non-continuous dream time in Philip O'Connor's sequence, as the continuous present in Robert Duncan's 'Coming out of' and 'Turning into', where after a few lines everything happens at once.

Mythological time that never ends waits behind the chimerical worlds evolving behind and before our eyes, 'stirring new freaks of vision there'. The rag-taggle impetuous prankster springs to spontaneous life inside Philip O'Connor while dessert arrives at his table. He destroys himself with laughter, and then eats his pudding.

United with all this is a lyricism, probably both most mysterious and most accessible when it speaks of a lover who opens into a universe of colours and vast space, the inspired, receptive regions of the mind:

### Lady Love

She is standing on my lids
And her hair is in my hair
She has the colour of my eye
She has the body of my hand
In my shade she is engulfed
As a stone against the sky

She will never close her eyes
And she does not let me sleep
And her dreams in the bright day
Make the suns evaporate
And me laugh cry and laugh
Speak when I have nothing to say

(Paul Éluard, translated in *This Quarter*, 1932)

The spirit of surrealism has become the spirit of modern poetry: the search for the marvellous; the desire to break through boundaries between subject and object, between desire and reality; the need to create a vision superior to the ugliness of contemporary civilization. Surrealism endures in its insistence on a vivification of language, so that pre-learned categories crumble, and desire can reveal the beauty that categories cannot. Poets believe in this beauty.

EDWARD B. GERMAIN

*Dublin,*
*New Hampshire,*
*July 1977*

# Selected Bibliography

Ashbery, John: 'Growing Up Surreal', *Art News*, Vol. 67, No. 3, May, 1968.

Breton, André: *Manifestoes of Surrealism*, trans. Richard Seaver and Helen R. Lane, Ann Arbor, University of Michigan Press, 1969.

Breton, André: *What is Surrealism?*, trans. David Gascoyne, London, Faber & Faber, 1936.

Breton, André: 'Limits Not Frontiers of Surrealism', in *Surrealism*, ed. Herbert Read.

Dali, Salvador: *The Metamorphosis of Narcissus*, trans. Francis Scarfe, New York, J. Levy, 1937.

Dali, Salvador: 'The Stinking Ass', trans. J. Bronowski, *This Quarter*, 5, No. 1, September, 1932.

Davies, Hugh Sykes: 'Biology and Surrealism', *International Surrealist Bulletin*, No. 4, 1936.

Gascoyne, David: *A Short Survey of Surrealism*, London, Cobden-Sanderson, 1936.

Gascoyne, David: 'Premier Manifeste anglais du surrealism (Fragment)', *Cahiers d'Art*, X, 1935.

Gascoyne, David: Response to questionnaire in *New Verse*, No. 11, October, 1934.

Raine, Kathleen: 'David Gascoyne and the Prophetic Role', *Sewanee Review*, LXXV, No. 2, Spring, 1967.

Ray, Charles Paul: *The Surrealist Movement in England*, Ph.D Dissertation, Columbia University, 1962; Ann Arbor, University Microfilms, Inc.

Read, Herbert (ed.): *Surrealism*, London, Faber & Faber, 1936 (with an Introduction by Herbert Read).

Rubin, William S.: *Dada, Surrealism, and their Heritage*, New York, The Museum of Modern Art, 1968.

# PART I

*From the Twenties to the Second World War*

# BRAVIG IMBS

born 1904

## The Wind Was There

### I

all was in flight
wild geese in the sky
snow from the sky flying
rivers hastening to the sea
and waves from the midsea
hastening to the shore

horses running from a fence
fences running from the ground
ground fleeing from the sky
and the sky was filled with flying stars
and suns innumerable

daisies springing from the grass
pines fleeing up the mountainside
even the mountain was in flight
less swift than southward geese
or rivers in the spring
less swift than these but fleeing still
stone upon stone scraping in slow erosion
gravel grinding into dust and fleeing before the wind

### II

all was in flight
even from a distance I
my flight was faster than a fleeing cloud
I only knew the wind was there
swift and imperious and proud
sharper than fine steel

### III

so shall I ever flee
swifter yet swifter
until the speed is such
my spirit shall enkindle with the wind
and then
a brown and crackled leaf I'll fall
my flesh to shrivel into mould
my blood to mingle with the seeping rain
and all my body's flight become a strange return

## Sleep

### I

slowly the ponderous doors of lead imponderous
pushed by a wedging force unthinking opened
how like a cloud I floated down the dim green air
unthinking of the soft violence of odorous winds
the falling plaint of hidden violins
and eyes
following

### II

doors unto doors unfolded downward
and I was like unto a sailing ship
stern downward sailing on a dim green sea
unmindful of the rich push of flowery winds
the melting voices of far seraphims
and arms
following

### III

slowly the ponderous doors of lead imponderous
lowered above my head in absolute slow closing
quiet as a shadow on a dim green wall
I rested in my dark and ivory vault
the violins were no more nor eyes nor arms
hours on hours
following

# PIERRE LOVING

1893–1950

## The Black Horse Rider

For George Anthell

Between them is the land of broken colors,
the land that makes a mock of him
with miles.
He rides, he rides,
he passes through the flat
chrome wheatfields
cut by the plough of the river makers.

The hills are aslant,
the clay torsos, the hills,
the clay has a red wound,
it gapes.
The white roots cry,
there is a mute susurrus in the dark:
poppies, poppies are you not
their pain?

With hoof on flint and flint
the black horse
rides: black wind, black
against fire.

The black horse crooks his
forelegs, the hills split open,
his nostrils pour flame.
Snort, snort through miles,
O charger, through rock.

He drinks the mezas,
he burns his thin knees over
braziers of grass:
Ride, ride.

Sky is spilt water,
a silver hello is flung
from star to star.
Black horse breaks
fire underfoot and now
his mane is a burnt city,
his mouth churned ocean,
foam on his belly a constellation.

At last he tramples
the sand
behemoth
Asleep before the sea.

# KENNETH FEARING

1902–1961

## *Evening Song*

Sleep, McKade.
    Fold up the day. It was a bright scarf.
    Put it away.
    Take yourself to pieces like a house of cards.

It is time to be a grey mouse under a tall building.
    Go there. Go there now.
    Look at the huge nails. Run behind the pipes.
    Scamper in the walls.
    Crawl towards the beckoning girl, her breasts are warm.
    But here is a dead man. A murderer?
    Kill him with your pistol. Creep past him to the girl.

Sleep, McKade.
    Throw one arm across the bed. Wind your watch.
    You are a gentleman, and important.
    Yawn. Go to sleep.

The continent turning from the sun is quiet.
    Your ticker waits for tomorrow morning
    And you are alive now.
    It will be a long time before they put McKade under the sod.
    Sometime, but not now.
    Sometime, though. Sometime, for certain.

Take apart your brain,
    Close the mouths in it that have been hungry,
    They are fed for a while.
    Go to sleep, you are a gentleman. McKade, alive and sane.
    A gentleman of position.

Tip your hat to the lady.
>   Speak to the mayor.
>   You are a personal friend of the mayor's, are you not?
>   True. A friend of the mayor's.
>   And you met the Queen of Roumania. True.

Then go to sleep.
>   Be a dog sleeping in the old sun.
>   Be a poodle drowsing in the old sun, by the Appian Way.
>   Be a dog lying the meadow watching soldiers pass on the road.
>   Chase after the woman who beckons.
>   Run from the policeman with the dagger. It will split your bones.
>   Be terrified.
>   Curl up and drowse on the pavement of Fifth Avenue in the
>       old sun.
>   Sleep, McKade.
>   Yawn.
>   Go to sleep.

# YVOR WINTERS

1900–1968

### The Precision

God spoke once in the dark: dead sound
in the dead silence. I turned
in my sleep.
     I slept and sank away.
Then breath by breath I rose
a rigid skeleton
of thought spread over all the
night maintained by faith alone afraid
to waken, nay, afraid to stir
in sleep.

     I, face to face
with my own image.

     Mine, Rock, thought, and
rock. Concrete the flesh – it lay
within me, turned, cold
in the living sheets.

Suspended on cold iron, branded on air.

# EMILY HOLMES COLEMAN

born 1899

### *The Liberator*

Keys turning
   rattling in the loose locks
     opening high the doors
that close again
like death-hours coming faster

the walls are white
and the line of beds is staring
all the bars go up and down
and none of them lead outward

    and leaping eyes
      and stiff limbs
     follow the crunch of the keys

I am powerful now
and I will break those that carry the keys
    with little hammers
    small hammers
    which you will make for me
     and hide in the porridge
I will break all their heads
    and lay them in neat rows
    and we shall wave high the keys
    and open wide a million doors
and all of us shall dance in the snow
and that poor woman in the spiral casket
shall warm a wooden doll to her dress
    and lean her hair in the fire

the grating shall be taken from about the fire
and the woman and the keys shall go within
all of us
shall
dance
within

# EDOUARD RODITI

born 1898

## Seance

The stranger walks into the dark room where the two men sit at the table and talk of travel. The stranger joins in the conversation, saying: 'I have also traveled' and the two men look up and seem surprised at his sudden appearance. In the corners of the ceiling there is a sound as of very swift wings, a muttering of motors, and a chattering of thin voices. The stranger disappears. His voice is heard first in this corner, then in that, until it fades away somewhere near the open window. Where the stranger stood the two men find a railway ticket to an unknown destination.

## Hand

Clouds darken the plain.

From all sides, the mountains of the horizon move forward; the plain shrinks, crumpled into valleys that grow deeper. The three rivers become torrents that flow swiftly in their cavernous beds towards those dark spots where they meet: the cities.

Then the sun again.

The mountains move back to the distant circular horizon; the valleys disappear, and the three rivers flow placidly in their scarcely perceptible beds of luminous sands. The cities glisten with their crystal walls and the hard light is reflected from house to house along the glass streets. Men no longer drag their dark-blue shadows like long chains that rattled on the opaque cobble stones. Silence of light: frozen wines of sound. No wind stirs, sleepily coiled around the towers that are transparent stems bearing the white flowers of clouds which float, vehicles for our pure thoughts, like water-lilies on the surface of a stream until they fade into the blue depth of space.

## Aurora Borealis

A crystallization of color spreads from the upper regions of the dark sky towards the trembling nipples of the waves. The feathering fringes of clouds fade behind pillars of green light. Transparent curtains tremble everywhere. In the arctic temple, the hidden Samson of light shakes the moon-green pillars of the night.

Color these crystals with sudden blood; it is dawn, or else the last consumptive saliva of the dying day. Heartless hard light!

In the crisp light of the frozen tinkling stars, no waters flow. The ice-stars are icebergs in this black ocean. When the green glass cathedrals crash, the light and the pillars of light and the green pillars of moon-green crystallized light are reflected through space and finally settle like sharp blades above the trembling nipples of the waves.

Samson moves in the glass cathedrals. Samson and the bull and Samson and the sun and the sun is the bull and Samson is the sun and is the bull.

Let crackling twigs of green-white light weave fantastic tree-patterns on the mirror of the sea. Let the deceptive sky celebrate the fall of its ice-cathedrals and its icebergs and its ice-stars when darkness hardens the black waters into the sullen black ice-pack of night.

Red Samson the arctic red sun is moving in the groves of green pillars. There is the red tinge of consumptive blood flickering behind the moon-green glass pillars of light. Blood of red Samson, red blood of Samson, the red thief is sprinkling blood on the slanting pillars of the falling sanctuary of light that is doomed to succumb soon to the black ice-pack of night. Then there will be night and,

suddenly thrust into dark night, the red sex of the Samson-
sun must later rise out of eastern whiteness and destroy the
night.

Then the pillars of the black shattered temple of night
glow with a white light and a red light of consumptive
blood, but again later comes night then again the same
Samson as the temples crash each time when the red thief
scatters blood on the pillars of the light or the pillars of the
night. And the thief is Samson and the red sun is Samson
and Samson is the thief and Samson is the sun.

## [ANDRÉ BRETON]

### 1896–1966

*Freedom of Love*

My wife with the hair of a wood fire
With the thoughts of heat lightning
With the waist of an hourglass
With the waist of an otter in the teeth of a tiger
My wife with the lips of a cockade and of a bunch of stars of the
     last magnitude
With the teeth of tracks of white mice on the white earth
With the tongue of rubbed amber and glass
My wife with the tongue of a stabbed host
With the tongue of a doll that opens and closes its eyes
With the tongue of an unbelievable stone
My wife with the eyelashes of strokes of a child's writing
With brows of the edge of a swallow's nest
My wife with the brow of slates of a hothouse roof
And of steam on the panes
My wife with shoulders of champagne
And of a fountain with dolphin-heads beneath the ice
My wife with wrists of matches
My wife with fingers of luck and ace of hearts

With fingers of mown hay
My wife with armpits of marten and of beechnut
And of Midsummer Night
Of privet and of an angelfish nest
With arms of seafoam and of riverlocks
And of a mingling of the wheat and the mill
My wife with legs of flares
With the movements of clockwork and despair
My wife with calves of eldertree pith
My wife with feet of initials
With feet of rings of keys and Java sparrows drinking
My wife with a neck of unpearled barley
My wife with a throat of the valley of gold
Of a tryst in the very bed of the torrent
With breasts of night
My wife with breasts of a marine molehill
My wife with breasts of the ruby's crucible
With breasts of the rose's spectre beneath the dew
My wife with the belly of an unfolding of the fan of days
With the belly of a gigantic claw
My wife with the back of a bird fleeing vertically
With a back of quicksilver
With a back of light
With a nape of rolled stone and wet chalk
And of the drop of a glass where one has just been drinking
My wife with hips of a skiff
With hips of a chandelier and of arrow-feathers
And of shafts of white peacock plumes
Of an insensible pendulum
My wife with buttocks of sandstone and asbestos
My wife with buttocks of swans' backs
My wife with buttocks of spring
With the sex of an iris
My wife with the sex of a mining-placer and of a platypus
My wife with a sex of seaweed and ancient sweetmeat
My wife with a sex of mirror
My wife with eyes full of tears
With eyes of purple panoply and of a magnetic needle

My wife with savanna eyes
My wife with eyes of water to be drunk in prison
My wife with eyes of wood always under the axe
My wife with eyes of water-level of level of air earth and fire

(*Translated from the French by Edouard Roditi*)

# EMANUEL CARNEVALI

1861–1930

## Queer Things

One nostril means latin,
The other means greek.

My legs will be
little steel rods,
which will continue
trotting after
I am dead.

My arms are
two useless limbs
when I stand on my head,
(Which I never do).

My mouth, too often open,
will be my despair –
clogged and sputtering
and drivelling, –
when I'll be very old (which
will never be)

I hate my head
My rotting head
which will never fall of itself
like any decent pear.
It has the intention
of flying up to the sky,
but it will always trail in the dust:
eating grime and dirt,
screaming erotic songs,
begging all the world
to enter in it.

# HARRY CROSBY

1898–1929

## *Firebrand*

What is your feeling about the revolutionary spirit of your age, as expressed, for instance, in such movements as communism, surrealism, anarchism?

The revolutionary spirit of our age (as expressed by communism, surrealism, anarchism, madness) is a hot firebrand thrust into the dark lantern of the world.

    In Nine Decades
a Mad Queen shall be born.

## *Vision*

    I exchange eyes with the Mad Queen

      the mirror crashes against my face and
bursts into a thousand suns
    al! over the city flags crackle and bang
    fog horns scream in the harbor
    the wind hurricanes through the window
    and I begin to dance the dance of the
Kurd Shepherds

    I stamp upon the floor
    I whirl like dervishes

colors revolve dressing and undressing
I lash them with my fury
stark white with iron black
harsh red with blue
marble green with bright orange
and only gold remains naked

columns of steel rise and plunge
emerge and disappear
pistoning in the river of my soul
    thrusting upwards
    thrusting downwards
    thrusting inwards
    thrusting outwards
     penetrating

  I roar with pain

black-footed ferrets disappear into holes

the sun tattooed on my back
begins to spin
    faster and faster
    whirring whirling
throwing out a glory of sparks
sparks shoot off into space
sparks into shooting stars
shooting stars collide with comets

    Explosions
   Naked Colors Explode
     into
   Red Disaster

I crash out through the
window naked, widespread
upon a
   Heliosaurus
I uproot an obelisk and plunge
it into the ink-pot of the
Black Sea
I write the word
    SUN

## Telephone Directory

| | | |
|---|---|---|
| Mad Queen Aeronautical Corporation . . | Cyclone | 3030 |
| Mad Queen Chemical Corporation . . | Gunpowder | 3328 |
| Mad Queen Company for the Manufacture of Hand Grenades . . . | Gunpowder | 8878 |
| Mad Queen Drug Store of Tonics and Stimulants . . . . . | Detonator . | 8808 |
| Mad Queen Dynamiting and Blasting Company . . . . . | Rackarock | 4196 |
| Mad Queen Express Elevators . . | Speedway | 7898 |
| Mad Queen Fireworks Corporation . . | Hurricane . | 1144 |
| Mad Queen Garage for Vandals of the Road . | Speedway . | 3984 |
| Mad Queen Hospital for Electrifying the Heart | Cyclone . | 5679 |
| Mad Queen Jazz Band. . . . . | Detonator . | 8814 |
| Mad Queen Laboratory for the Manufacture of Aphrodisiacs . . . . | Gunpowder | 0090 |
| Mad Queen Lighting and Fuel Corporation . | Gunpowder | 4301 |
| Mad Queen Manufacturers of High Explosives | Thunderbolt | 4414 |
| Mad Queen Racing Automobiles . . . | Speedway . | 6655 |
| Mad Queen Rum Distillery . . . . | Explosion . | 1152 |
| Mad Queen Skyscrapers . . . . | Hurricane . | 7444 |
| Mad Queen Society for the Vivisection of the Philistines . . . . | Thunderbolt | 8778 |
| Mad Queen Society of Incendiaries . . | Rackarock | 2254 |
| Mad Queen Steam Locomotive Company . | Speedway . | 1010 |
| Mad Queen Steam Roller Manufacturers . | Detonator | 1234 |
| Mad Queen Windmills and Weathervanes . | Hurricane . | 0164 |

# THOMAS McGREEVY

1893–1967

## *Homage to Hieronymus Bosch*

A woman with no face walked into the light;
A boy, in a brown-tree norfolk suit,
Holding on
Without hands
To her seeming skirt.

She stopped,
And he stopped,
And I, in terror, stopped, staring.

Then I saw a group of shadowy figures behind her.

It was a wild wet morning
But the little world was spinning on.

Liplessly, somehow, she addressed it:
*The book must be opened*
*And the park too.*

I might have tittered
But my teeth chattered
And I saw that the words, as they fell,
Lay, wriggling, on the ground.

There was a stir of wet wind
And the shadowy figures began to stir
When one I had thought dead
Filmed slowly out of his great effigy on a tomb near by
And they all shuddered
He bent as if to speak to the woman
But the nursery governor flew up out of the well of Saint Patrick,
Confiscated by his mistress,

And, his head bent,
Staring out over his spectacles,
And scratching the gravel furiously,
Hissed –
   The words went *pingg*! like bullets,
   Upwards, past his spectacles –
*Say nothing, I say, say nothing, say nothing*!
And he who had seemed to be coming to life
Gasped,
Began hysterically, to laugh and cry,
And, with a gesture of impotent and half-petulant despair,
Filmed back into his effigy again.

High above the Bank of Ireland
Unearthly music sounded,
Passing westwards.

Then, from the drains,
Small sewage rats slid out.
They numbered hundreds of hundreds, tens, thousands.
Each bowed obsequiously to the shadowy figures
Then turned and joined in a stomach dance with his brothers and
   sisters.
Being a multitude, they danced irregularly.
There was rat laughter,
Deeper here and there,
And occasionally she-rats grew hysterical.
The shadowy figures looked on, agonized.
The woman with no face gave a cry and collapsed.
The rats danced on her
And on the wriggling words
Smirking.
The nursery governor flew back into the well
With the little figure without hands in the brown-tree clothes.

# JOHN CROWE RANSOM

1888–1974

*Prelude to an Evening*

Do not enforce the tired wolf
Dragging his infected wound homeward
To sit tonight with the warm children
Naming the pretty kings of France.

The images of the invaded mind
Being as the monsters in the dreams
Of your most brief enchanted headful,
Suppose a miracle of confusion:

That dreamed and undreamt become each other
And mix the night and day of your mind;
And it does not matter your twice crying
From mouth unbeautied against the pillow

To avert the gun of the same old soldier;
For cry, cock-crow, or the iron bell
Can crack the sleep-sense of outrage,
Annihilate phantoms who were nothing.

But now, by our perverse supposal,
There is a drift of fog on your mornings;
You in your peignoir, dainty at your orange cup,
Feel poising round the sunny room

Invisible evil, deprived and bold.
All day the clock will metronome
Your gallant fear; the needles clicking,
The heels detonating the stair's cavern.

Freshening the water in the blue bowls
For the buck berries, with not all your love,
You shall be listening for the low wind,
The warning sibilance of pines.

You like a waning moon, and I accusing
Our too banded Eumenides,
While you pronounce Noes wanderingly
And smooth the heads of the hungry children.

# BERNARD GUTTERIDGE

born 1916

## Man into a Churchyard

He comes unknown and heard and stands there.
Breathes there hardly and hands grip
Flesh and walking stick. Skips over mounds
To land flat footed in a bowl of roses.

Flicks at the crazy gravestones
Spitting loud desires wood crosses for himself:
Heaves them up with laughter to hang them,
Dangling on the atheist's fig tree.

Handsprings through the open door,
Signs with a swastika on the visitors' book
And goes through the shut iron gate
With a pansy in his buttonhole.

# GEOFFREY GRIGSON

born 1905

### *Before a Fall*

And what was the big room he walked in?
   The big room he walked in,
   Over the smooth floor,
   Under the sky light,
   Was his own brain.

And what was it he admired there?
   He admired there
   The oval mirror.

And what was it the oval mirror showed him there?
   It showed him the roots
   Through the ceiling,
   The gross armchair, the bookcase
   Shuttered with glass,
   The Hymns bound in velvet,
   The porcelain oven,
   The giant egg cups,
   The hairy needles,
   And the silence –

   And the smell of smouldering dung
   Hung between the walls
   (Which were yellow as dandelion).

And how did he leave?
   On the smooth floor
   His neat feet jarred
   And his teeth grew down
   To his heart, and he slipped
   On the white stairhead –

Which ended?
   Which ended in coldness
   And darkness,
   Through which he fell
   (So they tell)
   With little hope, and slowly.

# KENNETH ALLOTT

1912–1973

## *The Statue*

I take you looking at the statue
the smile is yours and the stone is you
the stone is simple and the smile is playful
the smile is stolen and the stone is fallen
I ask you to stand and smile like that until
thinking you stone, time has forgotten you.
They say but really I forget

however picturesque
however figurative
whether so often and so quizzical
whoever it was crying in another voice ...
Let us sit like tailors. At least I am sure of this:
man or woman or beast I recall no face.

The night is kind so please to bend your arm
hide your head in the hollow of your arm
nobody will take you unawares, nobody
and nobody will take you unprepared
for time it is now to step out of time
and sleep will come as easy as kiss my hand
and you will find sleep kind.

Sleep has few terrors if we sleep like you
it is a cooling shower that falls on you
the water running through mirrors noiselessly
dreaming in doing things you dreamt to do.

But now all brawn Colossus straightens up
and stammers in the language of birds
and the sea goes mincing back into the sunset
strange to have lived so long upon this planet
daylight and moonlight, all the fun in the world.

# FRANCIS SCARFE

born 1911

## The Merry Window

The alabaster legs of the lonely woman
hang from the window like white ensigns
out of the laughing window like false teeth
sheets, flagstaffs, telescopes, rolls of music,
or you would say beheaded necks of swans
or the electric horns of factories
where foreign dreams are nightly fabricated.

Yearning for her coal once heaved in the seam
for her the sewers shrieked their way through London
and pigeons ate each other in the air.

But the deserted lady is frozen to the marrow
her heart has floated into her left leg
and her forked tongue asks in three languages
for a bassoon, a pyramid, and an egg.

All the white birds have flown out of her lips
the Polar Bear has eaten her left breast
her eyes are covered with yellow webs of dust,
in fact she is what a Saint would call abandoned
since even her own self has forgotten her.

## Ode in Honour

Evening is part of the jig-saw truth of her,
ply-wood ply-flesh, her insolent reply
blinding the ace with a straight shot to centre,
the woman's a delicate devil in twenty places
blander and blonder, tinder tenderly
setting the smiles on fire in men's faces.

On any evening gets you ready for dark
swathes and saves you for the magic carpet
spirits you anywhere anytime anyhow
over the bridges the tunnels the hills the foothills
the pools lakes oceans cataracts crystal floes
the mountains and fountains the antique windows of space,
the deserts orchards vineyards milky ways,
over pontoons and the silting tracks of moons
over the decks and the docks where the clocks
chime, anywhere anytime, anyhow, any fresh place.

Anywhere where winds blow and babies grow
where poor men wait for money in a row
where magnates buy and sell your heaven and hell,
anyhow whether the storm runs over the roof
or hollow tooth aches or gangrene takes the soul,
anytime when the sun splutters and throws shrapnel
between the legs of dead men and mad lovers,
she will be there to hold you by the cuff
to give you all her stock of luck or love.

With
two round lips and two round eyes
and two round ears and two round palms
and two round arms and two round thighs,
any child, any girl, any woman, any surprise.


### Kitchen Poem

#### An Elegy for Tristan Tȝara

In the hungry kitchen
The dog sings for its dinner.
The housewife is writing her poem
On top of the frigidaire
Something like this:

'Hear in the kitchen
The crows fly home
Into the red-robed trees
That walk across the sky.

Hear under the floor
The three fountains rising and
Trickling through the bridge
Into the sea of poems.'

In the kitchen the housemother
Pours soup for her thousand children
As her man eats his silence
And the dog swallows its poem.

In all the kitchens of Europe
The radio shouts good news:
'Millions have had no accident today –
All wars have come to an end –
An honest politician
In another country
Wants to become a plumber –
All men will be equal, next year –
Volcano vomits ice-cream –
A silent poem has been invented.'

In my holy kitchen
I draw the blinds of night
On the homes of sleep.
I hold the world in my palms.
Now that I am old
I can measure life with words.
There's a nightingale in my coffee.
My bread is buttered with memories.
Since the old woman died
I have two souls.

When I was small we had a lucky black cat.
We had a magic horse-shoe on the wall,
It was rusty and brought no luck
But fetched the fields into the kitchen
And made us not forget horses.

When you are old you make your own magic.
You speak oftener for the dead.
You move free in the wonderland of the past.
You invent a future on the other shore of death.
You must speak for the dead,
You are their rusty horse-shoe
In all the kitchens of the world,
Not the mug on the radio
But a thought rescued from the past.

    (There was love in the thin soup
    A bone some lentils and great love.
    My mother's hands were clouds.
    There was a bluebird in the gasjet
    When she bathed us by the kitchen fire.

    There will be no such soup again
    Nor such transcendent poverty.
    I have lost the treasure of poverty.
    The old woman is dead and buried
    In her wonderland of oblivion,
    But lives in my kitchen poem
    In this 'sentimental' aside.)

Now that I am an old man, I think in bed.
I think nothing. I think poems –
The metronome of sleeplessness and death,
The art of being deliberately alone and yet
A centre in the vortex of the world,
Feelings stretched drum-tight on the grid of thought
As your decaying flesh taut on its bones,

Sensations phantom ideas dreams, pinned bugs
On the living conveyor-belt of experience,
While in the poem you are everybody else,
Each poem merging into another construct,
All poems rationally absurd impermanent
———————————— DADA ————————————
There being no poem ever, no poet ever.
An old man in a kitchen, cooking words.


    I am no poet I am
    Lived by unfinishable poems,
    The horse-shoe hammered
    On the anvil of my brain.


I think nothing. The poems think me.
I do not often write them down,
Being a structuration of the unknowable
That dies upon the page,
My inward poems whispered for the dead
While the living bury the living
With foul political slogans.

    An owl is hooting in my poem
    Which sleep will end.

    Good night, poet of life,
    Be with me always.
    I give you my kitchen poem,
    Immortal TRISTAN.

# A. J. M. SMITH

born 1902

## *Political Intelligence*

Nobody said Apples for nearly a minute –
I thought I should die.
Finally, though, the second sardine
from the end, on the left,
converted a try.
(It brought down the house.
The noise was terrific.
I dropped my glass eye.)

Meanwhile Mr Baldwin
managed to make himself heard.
He looked sad
but with characteristic aplomb said
keep calm there is no cause for alarm.
Two soldiers' crutches had sexual intercourse
on the spot with a little bit of fluff
from a lint bandage in the firing chamber
of a 12 inch gun.
People agreed not to notice.
The band played a little bit louder.
It was all very British.

# NIALL MONTGOMERY

### *Eyewash*

EYES always open eyes
onions we were all found under
eyes never in a hurry wait for me
blink at the smash preserve the negative hold on a minute
(we are taking actuality as a section through sentiment at that
    point)

MICROPHONES tearing the remote controls controlling tears
twisting the tender cables urgent flowers suffer so
in evening close the door you can't come in
deface the setting sun when they is done
(three guggly waters play at hide and seek the moon what time is it)

CLOCK out important messages on his vanishing brain
rimless offerings to fear before he forgets
that formula for gratitude accumulating at compound interest
doubling itself measuring pulling that rolling drain that
their civil service filleted with nourishment

TWO of the girls I won't have to name
myopic charity and bitter shame
they will have the same again
at least one hopes to be buried at the current rate of exchange
with god the father in glasnevin or into dust in deansgrange

CROOKED smiles swell the anonymous elation quota
the park railings glazed from fellows leaning against them reflect
as the boys say an inability to adjust their suspenders quickly
    but why should she caress what she won't need
    sprung thighs splayed from the limp proscenium where
    the cost of living grins from hip to hip with

roses nuzzling in the apron goodness knows
  that dreams and crumples like a pregnant fool
Ah! Beauty, sprung from cardiac failure and ammoniated quinine
Hi-ya, baby! The verdict's justifiable suicide

I said piratic Jesuits with their ingrown eyes
Patrol all secret ways to Paradise

GIVE me a drink before I love you too
young man I easily must have met before
so sweaty are your teeth so green your hands
your voice crawling alive with home-grown poetry

ICE always opens up
taxiing off with data day and night
eyes panning trucking fading yourselves out
remembering the dry-throated black-board at school
(these things are all available to salvation they say)

# JOHN BEEVERS

1911–1975

*Atameros*

The palace with revolving doors was mine
And three of us went up its steps
To the tall room whose walls were made
Of the furred eyes of moths.

One only went within –
Atameros the Greek;
With steps that slid along the floor
He slipped inside and closed the door.

Whilst Williamson took off his boots,
Produced three large synthetic mandrake roots
And softly musicked Home Sweet Home
Upon his dirty pocket-comb.

Within the room a metal thread
Uncoiled to greet Atameros;
He placed his bowler-hat upon its head
And skated round and round
To the delightful sound

Of eight trombones,
Five saxophones,
And a lynched nigger's
Rattling bones.

Meanwhile, I hung out of the window and spat walnut-
shells into the sea breaking on the walls far below.

Two doors he tried
One opened wide
He saw his face inside.

Down the corridor he walked –
Sixteen stools behind him stalked –
Till he came where sponges grew:
Then Atameros really knew
Which end of the twig was forked.
This was the beach where the rats bred
So, reaching to the shelf above his head,
Atameros took the bowl
And strewed with seagulls' eyes
The crystal inches of the sand,
Setting them in a bloodshot squint
Towards the blue Madonna
Whose thighs nipped close the heavy clouds
Above that grey and troubled sea,
The soup of dead men's bones,
Which washed with long-whipped moan,
The stumpy coral teeth of Fraser's Bay.

But time was getting on.
Atameros took out his watch.
It fluttered from his hand
And minutes, like a cloud of nervous bats,
Brushed past him
As the eyes closed down their lids.

And I, still in my tower, lost vast sums at Crown and Anchor,
for I was competing with the sun and the mailed sword.

He spat and every globule turned to pearls
That in low-toned concentric whirls
Ran on before him
Till he came
To that high room without a name
Where all things shift
And yet remain the same.
On the black bed she lay
With little ants at play
About the lobe of each her ears,
Biting each minute three small fears.

Once every day they stopped,
Scoured the clanging skies
Caught all the turtle-doves
Tore off their heads
And from their beaks
Built her a tower
Which ringed the moon
With wide lassoes of bloody twittering tongues.
Her breasts were glass
Through them he gazed
And saw the beatings of her heart.

# GEORGE BARKER

born 1913

## Section VI from *Calamiterror*

### 1

Meandering abroad in the Lincolnshire meadows day
Day and day a month perhaps, lying at night lonely,
The early September evening administering a mystery,
The moon executing its wavering sleight of hand, I sense the
Advent of the extraordinary event, the calamiterror,
Turn and encounter the mountain descending upon me —
The moment of terror flashes like dead powder
Revealing the features of the mass as mine.

### 2

Time like a mountain made of my own shadow
Collapsing on me, buries me in my life.
It is the future, undermined by present,
Falling appallingly backward. I bring
The cracked escarpments hurling down, I catch
The agonised glint of years in a fall of
Rubble, the time clatters down with branches
I hear the broken life scream and sob like me.

### 3

Meandering abroad in the Lincolnshire meadows
Throw up no mountain featured with self's face.
Idling like Hylas beside the Babylonian stream
Admire the harp on the willow not the bright mask
Suspended through the depths or down
Internally and eternally drowned you go. I know.
I wandered at night admiring the moonlight mountain
The moon had made the monster of my own.

4

I see the elements of my growth were drawn
Not from the objects that encourage growth,
The mountain ornamented with morning tears,
The musical tree, the hesitating river,
But the distorted mountain of the bowels,
The hysterical tree that branches to the arms,
The lunar river from the sexual fountain.
Feeding on self, the internal cannibal
Stands like a gap over its swallowed self.

5

About the adult like the solar system
Objects revolve, holding the man in place.
The abdomen of youth is the balloon world
Twisted to fit between the ribs. The Spartan boy
Had his own fox-globe hidden at his belly.
The youth of sorrow mourns this indigestion,
The world swelling in his guts. I vomit.
This is the act that I now execute.

6

Why walk at night admiring the moonlight mountain,
It is to find and feel the real and fine.
More may the glittering angle indicate
The physiognomy of the divine than thine.
Who is the parent of the innumerable plant,
It is not the sweet onion hanging at my loin.
The green tree springing in the rear of space
Follows the Greek sun and not my face.

### 7

I recall how the rosetree sprang out of my breast.
I recall the myriads of birds in the cage of my head,
I recall my third finger the branch of myrtle,
I recall the imprisoned women wailing in my bowels.
I was the figure of the Surrealist Exhibition
With a mass of roses face. I hung like hawk
Hungry over the running world, I hung
Like sun that pulls the bright boys, like the spider.

### 8

I saw the moon nightly performing a circle about
The pivotal point of my eye. The bird flew
Either towards or from me, sang to me or was
Silent. I sensed the violent spinning of things, –
I was their axle like the polar tree.
The key of kings had fallen from the blue
Into my keyhole eye, I knew I knew.
I felt the crush of hell in my left side.

### 9

It was on Sunday the 12th April I saw
The figure of William Blake bright and huge
Hung over the Thames at Sonning. I had not had this.
Familiar with the spatial mathematic,
Acknowledging the element of matter,
I was acquainted with the make of things,
But not this. I had not acknowledged this.
I had not encountered prototype.

10

I saw William Blake large and bright like ambition,
Absolute, glittering, actual and gold.
I saw he had worlds and worlds in his abdomen,
And his bosom innumerably enpeopled with all birds.
I saw his soul like a cinema in each of his eyes,
And Swedenborg labouring like a dream in his stomach.
I remember the myrtle sprouting from his hand
And saw myself the minor bird on the bough.


11

I recognized the cosmology of the objects,
The contributing and constituting things,
Which contemplated too close make a chaos,
The glorious plethora, the paradise mass, the chaos of
Glory, in which the idiot wanders collecting.
I recognized the cosmology of chaos,
Observing that the condition rendering
Chaos cosmos is the external fact.


12

William Blake was larger than my Lincolnshire mountain
When like my mountain fell. I heard the catastrophic
Fragments of his torso breaking past me, it was
The object of the physical world breaking on me
Like Krakatoa like Krakatoa like the
Fist shooting out of the box like the gradual
Appearance of morning at morning like Tutankhamen
Carefully divesting itself in public places.

### 13

I achieved apocalypse – hearing slowly the sounds
Against which my ears had made their own music.
I heard first the Rhondda choral echo up the valley
Trying to find god's ear, I heard the presage
Ironically rumbling along the Channel, war:
The ancestral voice, the ancestral voice. And
I saw in a fog of gas Mr Baldwin orating:
We must repair the deficiencies of our forces.
I heard three women weeping in Irun's ruins.

### 14

Nothing I could not hear, *Berliner
Tageblatt*, *Daily Telegraph*, *L'Humanité*, *Isvestia*,
The air like newsboys shrieking, recounting
Instances of hate, of insult, aggravation, and
The Rhondda choral, the Durham hymn, over all.
I met seven saints in Salisbury with cotton wool in their ears,
I remembered with shame my own music.
The splitting of the central pillar like aural lightning,
I felt it crack my abdomen, the world.

*Poems from the Surrealist Group in London: Hugh Sykes
Davies to Roland Penrose*

# HUGH SYKES DAVIES

born 1909

## Music in an Empty House

The house was empty and
    the people of the house
    gone many months

Months for the weevil
    for the patient worm
    timber-mole softly tunnelling
    for the parliament
    of rats

Footsteps slink past
    damp walls
    down
    long
    corridors

Slow feet
    warily scuff
    bare boards
The much-bitten
    tapestry
      holds
        many
    moths

In a certain curtain'd room
    the halting steps evade
    chairs white shrouded

To twitch the winding-sheet
    around a grand piano
    thin phalanx of sound
    sharp rat's teeth edge yellow
    with decay

The much-bitten
    tapestry
    holds
    many
    moths

On rat's teeth-edge
    fingers preparate
    hesitate

Then falling send
  as tenantry
    damp-muffled chords
      rusting strings
  a still-born song

Their fortissimo    The tattered
  scarce                tapestry
  stirs                 holds
  near                 many
  cobwebs          moths

## Poem

In the stump of the old tree, where the heart has rotted out,
there is a hole the length of a man's arm, and a dank pool at the
bottom of it where the rain gathers, and the old leaves turn into
lacy skeletons. But do not put your hand down to see, because

in the stumps of old trees, where the hearts have rotted out,
there are holes the length of a man's arm, and dank pools at the
bottom where the rain gathers and old leaves turn to lace, and the
beak of a dead bird gapes like a trap. But do not put your
hand down to see, because

in the stumps of old trees with rotten hearts, where the rain
gathers and the laced leaves and the dead bird like a trap, there
are holes the length of a man's arm, and in every crevice of the
rotten wood grow weasel's eyes like molluscs, their lids open
and shut with the tide. But do not put your hand down to see,
because . . .

. . . in the stumps of old trees where the hearts have rotted out
there are holes the length of a man's arm where the weasels are
trapped and the letters of the rook language are laced on the
sodden leaves, and at the bottom there is a man's arm.
But do not put your hand down to see, because

in the stumps of old trees where the hearts have rotted out
there are deep holes and dank pools where the rain gathers, and
if you ever put your hand down to see, you can wipe it in
the sharp grass till it bleeds, but you'll never want
to eat with it again.


## Poem

It doesn't look like a finger it looks like a feather of broken glass
It doesn't look like something to eat it looks like something eaten
It doesn't look like an empty chair it looks like an old woman
    searching in a heap of stones
It doesn't look like a heap of stones it looks like an estuary where
    the drifting filth is swept to and fro on the tide
It doesn't look like a finger it looks like a feather with broken teeth
The spaces between the stones are made of stone
It doesn't look like a revolver it looks like a convolvulus
It doesn't look like a living convolvulus it looks like a dead one
KEEP YOUR FILTHY HANDS OFF MY FRIENDS
    USE THEM ON YOU BITCHES OR
YOURSELVES BUT KEEP THEM OFF MY
    FRIENDS
The faces between the stones are made of bone

It doesn't look like an eye it looks like a bowl of rotten fruit

It doesn't look like my mother in the garden it looks like my father when he came up from the sea covered with shells and tangle

It doesn't look like a feather it looks like a finger with broken wings

It doesn't look like the old woman's mouth it looks like a handful of broken feathers or a revolver buried in cinders

The faces beneath the stones are made of stone

It doesn't look like a broken cup it looks like a cut lip

It doesn't look like yours it looks like mine

BUT IT IS YOURS NOW

SOON IT WILL LOOK LIKE YOURS

AND ANYTHING YOU SEE WILL BE USED AGAINST YOU

# DAVID GASCOYNE

born 1916

## *And the Seventh Dream is the Dream of Isis*

I

white curtains of infinite fatigue
dominating the starborn heritage of the colonies of St Francis
white curtains of tortured destinies
inheriting the calamities of the plagues of the desert
encourage the waistlines of women to expand
and the eyes of men to enlarge like pocket-cameras
teach children to sin at the age of five
to cut out the eyes of their sisters with nail-scissors
to run into the streets and offer themselves to unfrocked priests
teach insects to invade the deathbeds of rich spinsters
and to engrave the foreheads of their footmen with purple signs
for the year is open the year is complete
the year is full of unforeseen happenings
and the time of earthquakes is at hand

today is the day when the streets are full of hearses
and when women cover their ring fingers with pieces of silk
when the doors fall off their hinges in ruined cathedrals
when hosts of white birds fly across the ocean from america
and make their nests in the trees of public gardens
the pavements of cities are covered with needles
the reservoirs are full of human hair
fumes of sulphur envelop the houses of ill-fame
out of which bloodred lilies appear.

across the square where crowds are dying in thousands
a man is walking a tightrope covered with moths

## 2

there is an explosion of geraniums in the ballroom of the hotel
there is an extremely unpleasant odour of decaying meat
arising from the depetalled flower growing out of her ear
her arms are like pieces of sandpaper
or wings of leprous birds in taxis
and when she sings her hair stands on end
and lights itself with a million little lamps like glowworms
you must always write the last two letters of her christian name
upside down with a blue pencil

she was standing at the window clothed only in a ribbon
she was burning the eyes of snails in a candle
she was eating the excrement of dogs and horses
she was writing a letter to the president of france

## 3

the edges of leaves must be examined through microscopes
in order to see the stains made by dying flies
at the other end of the tube is a woman bathing her husband
and a box of newspapers covered with handwriting
when an angel writes the word TOBACCO across the sky
the sea becomes covered with patches of dandruff
the trunks of trees burst open to release streams of milk
little girls stick photographs of genitals to the windows of their
     homes
prayerbooks in churches open themselves at the death service
and virgins cover their parents' beds with tealeaves
there is an extraordinary epidemic of tuberculosis in yorkshire
where medical dictionaries are banned from the public libraries
and salt turns a pale violet colour every day at seven o'clock
when the hearts of troubadours unfold like soaked mattresses
when the leaven of the gruesome slum-visitors
and the wings of private airplanes look like shoeleather
shoeleather on which pentagrams have been drawn
shoeleather covered with vomitings of hedgehogs

shoeleather used for decorating wedding-cakes
and the gums of queens like glass marbles
queens whose wrists are chained to the walls of houses
and whose fingernails are covered with little drawings of flowers
we rejoice to receive the blessing of criminals
and we illuminate the roofs of convents when they are hung
we look through a telescope on which the lord's prayer has been
    written
and we see an old woman making a scarecrow
on a mountain near a village in the middle of spain
we see an elephant killing a stag-beetle
by letting hot tears fall onto the small of its back
we see a large cocoa-tin full of shapeless lumps of wax
there is a horrible dentist walking out of a ship's funnel
and leaving behind him footsteps which make noises
on account of his accent he was discharged from the sanatorium
and sent to examine the methods of cannibals
so that wreaths of passion-flowers were floating in the darkness
giving terrible illnesses to the possessors of pistols
so that large quantities of rats disguised as pigeons
were sold to various customers from neighbouring towns
who were adepts at painting gothic letters on screens
and at tying up parcels with pieces of grass
we told them to cut off the buttons on their trousers
but they swore in our faces and took off their shoes
whereupon the whole place was stifled with vast clouds of smoke
and with theatres and eggshells and droppings of eagles
and the drums of the hospitals were broken like glass
and glass were the faces in the last looking-glass.

## The End is Near the Beginning

Yes you have said enough for the time being
There will be plenty of lace later on
Plenty of electric wool
And you will forget the eglantine
Growing around the edge of the green lake
And if you forget the colour of my hands
You will remember the wheels of the chair
In which the wax figure resembling you sat

Several men are standing on the pier
Unloading the sea
The device on the trolly says MOTHER'S MEAT
Which means *Until the end.*

## The Cubical Domes

Indeed indeed it is growing very sultry
The indian feather pots are scrambling out of the room
The slow voice of the tobacconist is like a circle
Drawn on the floor in chalk and containing ants
And indeed there is a shoe upon the table
And indeed it is as regular as clockwork
Demonstrating the variability of the weather
Or denying the existence of manu altogether
For after all why should love resemble a cushion
Why should the stumbling-block float up towards the ceiling
And in our attic it is always said
That this is a sombre country the wettest place on earth
And then there is the problem of living to be considered
With its vast pink parachutes full of underdone mutton
Its tableaux of the archbishops dressed in their underwear
Have you ever paused to consider why grass is green
Yes greener at least it is said than the man in the moon
Which is why

The linen of flat countries basks in the tropical sun
And the light of the stars is attracted by transparent flowers
And at last is forgotten by both man and beast
By helmet and capstan and mesmerised nun
For the bounds of my kingdom are truly unknown
And its factories work all night long
Producing the strongest canonical wastepaper-baskets
And ant-eaters' skiing-shoes
Which follow the glistening murders as far as the pond
And then light a magnificent bonfire of old rusty nails
And indeed they are paid by the state for their crimes
There is room for them all in the conjuror's musical-box
There is still enough room for even the hardest of faces
For faces are needed to stick on the emperor's walls
To roll down the stairs like a party of seafaring christians
Whose hearts are on fire in the snow.


*Salvador Dali*


The face of the precipice is black with lovers;
The sun above them is a bag of nails; the spring's
First rivers hide among their hair.
Goliath plunges his hand into the poisoned well
And bows his head and feels my feet walk through his brain.
The children chasing butterflies turn round and see him there
With his hand in the well and my body growing from his head,
And are afraid. They drop their nets and walk into the wall like
    smoke.


The smooth plain with its mirrors listens to the cliff
Like a basilisk eating flowers.
And the children, lost in the shadows of the catacombs,
Call to the mirrors for help:
'Strong-bow of salt, cutlass of memory,
Write on my map the name of every river.'

A flock of banners fight their way through the telescoped forest
And fly away like birds towards the sound of roasting meat.
Sand falls into the boiling rivers through the telescopes' mouths
And forms clear drops of acid with petals of whirling flame.
Heraldic animals wade through the asphyxia of planets,
Butterflies burst from their skins and grow long tongues like plants,
The plants play games with a suit of mail like a cloud.

Mirrors write Goliath's name upon my forehead,
While the children are killed in the smoke of the catacombs
And lovers float down from the cliffs like rain.


## Yves Tanguy

The worlds are breaking in my head
Blown by the brainless wind
That comes from afar
Swollen with dusk and dust
And hysterical rain

The fading cries of the light
Awaken the endless desert
Engrossed in its tropical slumber
Enclosed by the dead grey oceans
Enclasped by the arms of the night

The worlds are breaking in my head
Their fragments are crumbs of despair
The food of the solitary damned
Who await the gross tumult of turbulent
Days bringing change without end.

The worlds are breaking in my head
The fuming future sleeps no more
For their seeds are beginning to grow
To creep and to cry midst the
Rocks of the deserts to come

Planetary seed
Sown by the grotesque wind
Whose head is so swollen with rumours
Whose hands are so urgent with tumours
Whose feet are so deep in the sand.


## 'The Truth is Blind'

The light fell from the window and the day was done
Another day of thinking and distractions
Love wrapped in its wings passed by and coal-black Hate
Paused on the edge of the cliff and dropped a stone
From which the night grew like a savage plant
With daggers for its leaves and scarlet hearts
For flowers – then the bed
Rose clocklike from the ground and spread its sheets
Across the shifting sands

Autumnal breath of mornings far from here
A star veiled in grey mist
A living man:

The snapping of a dry twig was his only announcement. The two
men, who had tied their boat to a branch that grew out over the
water's edge, and were now moving up through the rank tropical
vegetation, turned sharply.

He raised his eyes and saw the river's source
Between their legs – he saw the flaming sun
He saw the buildings in between the leaves
Behind their heads that were as large as globes
He heard their voices indistinct as rain
As faint as feathers falling
  And he fell

The boat sailed on
The masts were made of straw
The sails were made of finest silken thread
And out of holes on either side the prow
Gushed endless streams of water and of flame
In which the passengers saw curious things:

The conjurer, we are told, 'took out of his bag a silken thread,
and so projected it upwards that it stuck fast in a certain cloud of
air. Out of the same receptacle he pulled a hare, that ran away up
along the thread; a little beagle, which when it was slipped at the
hare pursued it in full cry; last of all a small dogboy, whom he
commanded to follow both hare and hound up the thread. From
another bag that he had he extracted a winsome young woman, at
all points well adorned, and instructed her to follow after hound
and dogboy.'

She laughed to see them gazing after her
She clapped her hands and vanished in thin air
To reappear upon the other bank
Among the restless traffic of the quays
Her silhouette against the dusty sky
Her shadow falling on the hungry stones
Where sat the pilot dressed in mud-stained rags

He knocked the fragile statue down
And ate her sugar head
And then the witnesses all gathered round
And pointed at the chasm at his feet:

Clouds of blue smoke, sometimes mixed with black, were being
emitted from the exhaust pipe. The smoke was of sufficient density
to be an annoyance to the driver following the vehicle or to
pedestrians.

The whispering of unseen flames
A sharp taste in the mouth.

## The Cage

In the waking night
The forests have stopped growing
The shells are listening
The shadows in the pools turn grey
The pearls dissolve in the shadow
And I return to you

Your face is marked upon the clockface
My hands are beneath your hair
And if the time you mark sets free the birds
And if they fly away towards the forest
The hour will no longer be ours

Ours is the ornate birdcage
The brimming cup of water
The preface to the book
And all the clocks are ticking
All the dark rooms are moving
All the air's nerves are bare.

Once flown
The feathered hour will not return
And I shall have gone away.

# [HANS ARP]

1887–1966

## *The Domestic Stones*

*(fragment)*

The feet of morning the feet of noon and the feet of evening
walk ceaselessly round pickled buttocks
on the other hand the feet of midnight remain motionless
in their echo-woven baskets

consequently the lion is a diamond

on the sofas made of bread
are seated the dressed and the undressed
the undressed hold leaden swallows between their toes
the dressed hold leaden nests between their fingers
at all hours the undressed get dressed again
and the dressed get undressed
and exchange the leaden swallows for the leaden nests

consequently the tail is an umbrella

a mouth opens within another mouth
and within this mouth another mouth
and within this mouth another mouth
and so on without end
it is a sad perspective
which adds an I-don't-know-what
to another I-don't-know-what

consequently the grasshopper is a column

the pianos with heads and tails
place pianos with heads and tails
on their heads and their tails

consequently the tongue is a chair

(*Translated from the French by David Gascoyne*)

## [ANDRÉ BRETON]

### 1896–1966

### *Postman Cheval*

We are the birds always charmed by you from the top of these
    belvederes
And that each night form a blossoming branch between your
    shoulders and the arms of your well beloved wheelbarrow
Which we tear out swifter than sparks at your wrist
We are the sighs of the glass statue that raises itself on its elbow
    when man sleeps
And shining holes appear in his bed
Holes through which stags with coral antlers can be seen in a glade
And naked women at the bottom of a mine
You remembered then you got up you got out of the train
Without glancing at the locomotive attacked by immense baro-
    metric roots
Complaining about its murdered boilers in the virgin forest
Its funnels smoking jacinths and moulting blue snakes
Then we went on, plants subject to metamorphosis
Each night making signs that man may understand
While his house collapses and he stands amazed before the singular
    packing-cases
Sought after by his bed with the corridor and the staircase
The staircase goes on without end
It leads to a millstone door it enlarges suddenly in a public square
It is made of the backs of swans with a spreading wing for banisters
It turns inside out as though it were going to bite itself
But no, it is content at the sound of our feet to open all its steps
    like drawers
Drawers of bread drawers of wine drawers of soap drawers of ice
    drawers of stairs
Drawers of flesh with handsfull of hair
Without turning round you seized the trowel with which breasts
    are made

We smiled at you you held us round the waist
And we took the positions of your pleasure
Motionless under our lids for ever as woman delights to see man
After having made love.

(*Translated from the French by David Gascoyne*)


[ANDRÉ BRETON]


## The Spectral Attitudes

I attach no importance to life
I pin not the least of life's butterflies to importance
I do not matter to life
But the branches of salt the white branches
All the shadow bubbles
And the sea-anemones
Come down and breathe within my thoughts
They come from tears that are not mine
From steps I do not take that are steps twice
And of which the sand remembers the flood-tide
The bars are in the cage
And the birds come down from far above to sing before these bars
A subterranean passage unites all perfumes
A woman pledged herself there one day
This woman became so bright that I could no longer see her
With these eyes which have seen my own self burning
I was then already as old as I am now
And I watched over myself and my thoughts like a nightwatchman
    in an immense factory
Keeping watch alone
The circus always enchants the same tramlines
The plaster figures have lost nothing of their expression
They who bit the smile's fig

I know of a drapery in a forgotten town
If it pleased me to appear to you wrapped in this drapery
You would think that your end was approaching
Like mine
At last the fountains would understand that you must not say
    Fountain
The wolves are clothed in mirrors of snow
I have a boat detached from all climates
I am dragged along by an ice-pack with teeth of flame
I cut and cleave the wood of this tree that will always be green
A musician is caught up in the strings of his instrument
The skull and crossbones of the time of any childhood story
Goes on board a ship that is as yet its own ghost only
Perhaps there is a hilt to this sword
But already there is a duel in this hilt
During the duel the combatants are unarmed
Death is the least offence
The future never comes

The curtains that have never been raised
Float to the windows of houses that are to be built
The beds made of lilies
Slide beneath the lamps of dew
There will come an evening
The nuggets of light become still underneath the blue moss
The hands that tie and untie the knots of love and of air
Keep all their transparency for those who have eyes to see
They see the palms of hands
The crowns in eyes
But the brazier of crown and palms
Can scarcely be lit in the deepest part of the forest
There where the stags bend their heads to examine the years
Nothing more than a feeble beating is heard
From which sound a thousand louder or softer sounds proceed
And the beating goes on and on
There are dresses that vibrate
And their vibration is in unison with the beating

When I wish to see the faces of those that wear them
A great fog rises from the ground
At the bottom of the steeples behind the most elegant reservoirs
    of life and of wealth
In the gorges which hide themselves between two mountains
On the sea at the hour when the sun cools down
Those who make signs to me are separated by stars
And yet the carriage overturned at full speed
Carries as far as my last hesitation
That awaits me down there in the town where the statues of bronze
    and of stone have changed places with statues of wax
Banyans banyans.

(*Translated from the French by David Gascoyne*)

## [SALVADOR DALI]

born 1904

### *The Art of Picasso*

the biological
and dynastic phenomenon
which constitutes the cubism
of
Picasso
has been
the first great imaginative cannibalism
surpassing the experimental ambitions
of modern mathematical
physics.

\*     \*     \*

The life of Picasso
will form the polemic basis
as yet misunderstood

according to which
physical psychology
will open up anew
a niche of living flesh
and of darkness
for philosophy.

\*     \*     \*

For because
of the materialist
anarchic
and systematic thought
of
Picasso
we shall be able to know physically
experimentally
and without need
of the new psychological 'problematics'
of kantian savour
of the gestaltists
all the misery
of
localized and comfortable
objects of consciousness
with their lazy atoms
sensations infinite
and
diplomatic.

\*     \*     \*

For the hyper-materialist thought
of Picasso
proves
that the cannibalism of the race
devours
'the intellectual species'
that the regional wine
already moistens
the family trouser-flap

of the phenomenologist mathematics
of
the future
that there exist extra-psychological
'strict appearances'
intermediary between
imaginative grease
and
monetary idealisms
between
passed-over arithmetics
and sanguinary mathematics
between the 'structural' entity
of an 'obsessing sole'
and the conduct of living things
in contact with the 'obsessing sole'
for the sole in question
remains
totally exterior
to the comprehension
of
the
gestalt-theory
this theory of the strict
appearance
and of the structure
does not possess
physical means
permitting
analysis
or even
the registration
of human behaviour
vis-à-vis
with structures
and appearances
presenting themselves objectively

as
physically delirious
for
there does not exist
in our time
as far as I know
a physics
of psycho-pathology
a physics of paranoia
which can only be considered
as
the experimental basis
of the coming philosophy
of
psycho-pathology
of the coming
philosophy of 'paranoiac-critical' activity
which one day
I shall try to envisage polemically
if I have the time
and the inclination.

(*Translated from the Spanish by David Gascoyne*)

[BENJAMIN PÉRET]

1899–1958

## The Staircase with a Hundred Steps

The blue eagle and the demon of the steppes
in the last cab in Berlin
Legitimate defence
of lost souls
the red mill at the beggars' school
awaits the poor student

With the housemaid Know huntsmen how to hunt
on pay-day
Know huntsmen how to hunt
as papa speculates
with the smile
By the dagger the dagger the dagger
the tiger of the seas dreams of happiness
Avenged
The vestal virgin of the Ganges cries out Vanity
when the flesh succumbs
Stop look and listen
the famous turkey spends a day of pleasure
turning round in an enchanted circle
with the pluck of a lion
M'sieur the major
My Paris
my uncle from America
my heart and my legs
slaves of beauty
admire the conquests of Nora
while someone asks for a typewriter
for the black pirate
It is not possible
that a woman dressed as the *Merry Widow*
could become the wind's prey
because the millionairess Madame Sans-Gene
leads a wild existence
in another's skin
Her son was right
Patrol-leader 129 who wears an Italian straw-hat
and is the ace of jockeys
is abandoning a little adventuress
for a woman
It is the April-Moon which chases the buffalo
to Notre-Dame of Paris
Oh what a bore the indomitable man
with clear eyes
wishes to judge him by the law of the desert

but the lovers with children's souls have gone away
Ah what a lovely voyage

(*Translated from the French by David Gascoyne*)


[BENJAMIN PÉRET]


*Making Feet and Hands*

Eye standing up eye lying down eye sitting

Why wander about between two hedges made of stair-rails
while the ladders become soft
as new-born babes
as zouaves who lose their homeland with their shoes
Why raise one's arms towards the sky
since the sky has drowned itself
without rhyme or reason
to pass the time and make its moustaches grow
Why does my eye sit down before going to bed
because saddles are making donkeys sore
and pencils break in the most unpredictable fashion
the whole time
except on stormy days
when they break into zigzags
and snowy days
when they tear their sweaters to pieces
But the spectacles the old tarnished spectacles
sing songs while gathering grass for cats
The cats follow the procession
carrying flags
flags and ensigns
The fish's tail crossing a beating heart
the throat regularly rising and falling to imitate the sea
   surrounding it

and the fish revolving about a ventilator
There are also hands
long white hands with nails of fresh greenery
and finger-joints of dew
swaying eyelashes looking at butterflies
saddened because the day made a mistake on the stairs
There are also sexes fresh as running water
which leap up and down in the valley
because they are touched by the sun
They have no beards but they have clear eyes
and they chase dragonflies
without caring what people will say

(*Translated from the French by David Gascoyne*)

[PABLO PICASSO]

1881–1973

*Poems*

hasten on your childhood to the hour when white in
memory blue borders white in its eyes very white and piece
of indigo of silver the glances white cross cobalt the white
paper that blue ink tears bluish away ultramarine descends
that white may rest troubled blue in dark green wall green
that writes its pleasure rain green clear that swims green
yellow in the clear oblivion at the edge of its green foot the
sand earth song sand of the earth afternoon sand earth

*

in the corner a violet jug the bells the folds of paper a
metal sheep life stretching out the paper a rifle shot the
paper rings the canaries in the shade white almost pink a
river in the white space in the clear blue shade of colours
lilac a hand at the edge of the shade makes of the shade in
the hand a very rose-coloured grasshopper a root lifts its
head a nail the block of the trees with nothing else a fish a
nest the heat in full light looks at a sunshade light the
fingers in the light the white of the paper the sun light in
the white cuts out a sparkling eyeshade the sun's light the
very white sun the intensely white sun

\*

in secret
be quiet say nothing
except the street be full of stars
and the prisoners eat doves
and the doves eat cheese
and the cheese eats words
and the words eat bridges
and the bridges eat looks
and the looks eat cups full of kisses in the *orchata*
that hides all with its wings
the butterfly the night
in a cafe last summer
in Barcelona

(*Translated from the French by David Gascoyne*)

## [GEORGES RIBEMONT-DESSAIGNES]

born 1884

### *Sliding Trombone*

I have a little windmill on my head
Which draws up water to my mouth and eyes
When I am hungry or moved to tears
I have a little horn full of the odour of absinth in my ears
And on my nose a green parakeet that flaps its wings
And cries 'Aux Armes'
When from the sky fall the seeds of the sun
The absence from the heart of steel
At the bottom of the boneless and stagnant realities
Is partial to crazy sea-fish
I am the captain and the alsatian at the cinema
I have in my belly a little agricultural machine
That reaps and binds electric flex
The cocoanuts thrown by the melancholy monkey
Fall like spittle into the water
Where they blossom again as petunias
I have in my stomach an ocarina and I have virginal faith
I feed my poet on the feet of a pianist
Whose teeth are even and uneven
And sad Sunday evenings
I throw my morganatic dreams
To the loving turtle-doves who laugh like hell.

(*Translated from the French by David Gascoyne*)

## [PIERRE UNIK]

### The Manless Society

Morning trickles over the bruised vegetables
like a drop of sweat over the lines of my hand
I crawl over the ground
with stern and wrinkled mouth
the sun swells into the canals of monstrous leaves
which recover cemeteries harbours houses
with the same sticky green zeal
then with disturbing intensity there passes through my mind
the absurdity of human groupings
in these lines of closely packed houses
like the pores of the skin
in the poignant void of terrestrial space
I hear the crying of birds of whom it used to be said
that they sang and implacable resembled stones
I see flocks of houses munching the pith of the air
factories which sing as birds once sang
roads which lose themselves in harvests of salt
pieces of sky which become dry on verdigris moss
a pulley's creaking tells us that a bucket rises in a well
it is full of limpid blood
which evaporates in the sun
nothing else will trouble this circuit on the ground
until evening
which trembles under the form of an immense pinned butterfly
at the entrance of a motionless station.

(*Translated from the French by David Gascoyne*)

# GEORGE REAVEY

born 1907

## Dismissing Progress and its Progenitors

Their minds are so frail the least squeak upsets them
of mice in the pantry or bats in the belfry
but a growl or a howl a belch or a bellow
will drive them to bedlam for fear of stigma
Their bellies boil over with brisk indignation
as soon as you mention a truth in a hundred
while love and all its accessories
fills them with imperative peregrination
Squeamish till beer makes them a cesspool of wit
these are my brethren in sabbath attire
room for moths only and larvae
A poet's their terror their ghost in a garret
an ill-starred astrologer mad on the pavement
to throw eggs at smirk over be vague and gregarious
but never gregorian never egregious

They increase to assess and assess to increase
by secret enactments of lust and mistrust
They grow and aspire to a kind of flat-ironed eternity
till some cataclysm boots them into lasting oblivion
So when they would give me candy or sugar
the foot of my verse is the knell of their hearse

GEORGE REAVEY

*'How many fires'*

How many fires
   what horizons
strangeness of the sky
   human face stranger
Where shall I stake
   the flame of my hands
where stay a firebrand heart
   in its nomad blaze

# ROGER ROUGHTON

1916–1941

*Soluble Noughts and Crosses; or,*
*California, Here I Come*

to E.A.

In a small theodolite of paper
I could see the eyelash of a girl,
The most beautiful young girl of all,
Who was only dressed in cellophane,
Who was speaking from a stone
And saying this to me:
'Look out for the red and written triangle,
And enclose a penny-halfpenny stamp;
For I must go at ten to one,
Ten to one it's guineas time,
Ten to one will be too many,
Ten to one you'll come in last.
Yes, did you hear:
My fingers hang like pictures,
And my breasts are pointing to the North?'

So I made an expedition to the Pole,
While thin birds flew off sideways with a sob;
There I heard a ringing at the door,
Where some gongs were waiting in a queue;
I played them all in turn
And presently she stepped out from a handbag,
Saying this to me:
'The happy compass is decided,
I must come at ten to one,
Ten to one's beginner's time,
Ten to one won't be enough,
Ten to one we'll get there first.
Please take this down,

Yes take this down, for purple trees will sing the answer,
For rhyming trains are meeting at a foxtrot,
For string is floating on the water,
For we are opening a parcel meant for both;
Yes please take this down, for living words are played together,
For love has grown up like a hair.'


## Building Society Blues

The vultures are being spring-cleaned,
That anonymous letter came from you-know-who;
The hawker who sold you the dangerous toy:
He meant business too.

Do you want to become an Insoluble Crime,
A lynching held in one of the parks?
You would certainly cry, though your hand were held tight
By Man Mountain Marx.

Will you cross your desires and your heart,
Finding reprieve in a suitable mass?
The Maxims they use are not to your taste,
Nor is the incense gas.

Dare you ask for a rifle and sign on the line?
Remember the pain when you fractured your wrist.
Could you bear the damp air in the grave,
Or going to bed unkissed?

Maneating plants have grown out of the bath,
The pipes are about to burst through;
Can you call for the plumber to help, with his soviet
Grammar and tickle too?

# RUTHVEN TODD

born 1914

### Paul Klee

The small man suffers the indignities of childhood,
And is made to walk under ladders and caught
By the blind of darkness in the cat tormented night.
He is terrified by mice and sickened by blood;
Wolf-fanged horses chase after him along the road
And the tight-rope that he walks will always sag
When he has reached the centre so that his soft leg
Is pierced by the pine-needles of the magic wood.

And yet, in the middle of the formal garden,
He finds time to play at noughts and crosses,
And he is master of the sharp wasp whose burden
Of pollen fertilises the tall elaborate grasses.
In the enchanted ponds are luminous fishes
And paper-boats with cargoes of his wishes.

### Poem

I walk at dawn across the hollow hills,
Throwing egg-shells at the little moon.
Explosive for my bombs are puffball spores,
Measured out carefully, with a silver spoon.

Up there the heavy artillery is banked
To resist the bee that booms along the valley;
Machine-gun nests are placed among the crags
In case the eagles dare to make a sally.

Single-seater planes engage the curlew
Circling above the peat-moss and bog-myrtle.
The wound the old tup got an hour ago
Has since, I regretfully state, proved fatal.

Luckily the blind-worm does good work
And dodges past the enemy's best scout;
He rallies the wethers and attacks their rear,
Turning their predicted victory to a rout.

I walk at evening on the shattered moors,
Placing tea-leaves on the ancient cairns
In memory of the old tup and the dead plover.
I walk at midnight on the trampled ferns.


## Joan Miró

Once there were peasant pots and a dry brown hare
Upon the olive table in that magic farm;
Once all the showmen were blown about the fair
And none of them took hurt or any harm;
Once a man set his fighting bull to graze
In the strict paths of the forgotten maze.

This was that man who knew the secret line
And the strange shapes that went
In dreams; his was the bewitched vine
And the crying dog in the sky's tent.

Once he had a country where the sun shone
Through the enchanted trees like lace,
But now it is troubled and happiness is gone
For the bombs fell in that fine place
And the magician found when he had woken
His people dead, his gay pots broken.

(1937)

## Joan Miró

After that war, when death had gone away
About his other business – for many others
Had sent him invitations to come out to play
As, after all, both he and sleep were brothers –

The painter was haunted by the shapes of war;
His faces recognized those fearsome birds
Whose monolithic beaks forever tore
The hearts of men whose salt blood curds

When death goes jaunting round the sky
And time pauses, while they all must wait
That sudden moment when no piteous cry
Postpones the arrival of the promised date.

And, while the terror piled its years on years,
The artist filled his space with dreams
Which might be forecasts of his fears
For a world that did not hear the screams

Of those for whom death always could
Reach out beyond the Catalan farm,
The Dutch kitchen and the enchanted wood;
Through these sanctuaries extend his ugly arm.

(1947)

# HUMPHREY JENNINGS

1907–1951

*Prose Poem*

As the sun declined the snow at our feet reflected the most delicate
peach-blossom.

As it sank the peaks to the right assumed more definite, darker and
more gigantic forms.

The hat was over the forehead, the mouth and chin buried in the
brown velvet collar of the greatcoat. I looked at him wondering
if my grandfather's eyes had been like those.

While the luminary was vanishing the horizon glowed like copper
from a smelting furnace.

When it had disappeared the ragged edges of the mist shone like
the inequalities of a volcano.

Down goes the window and out go the old gentleman's head and
shoulders, and there they stay for I suppose nearly nine minutes.

Such a sight, such a chaos of elemental and artificial lights I never
saw nor expect to see. In some pictures I have recognized
similar effects. Such are *The Fleeting Hues of Ice* and *The Fire*
which we fear to touch.

# CHARLES MADGE

born 1912

## Poem

The walls of the maelstrom are painted with trees
And Napoleon's charger draws up at the filling-station,
Asking the way. Round they go, terribly late
To a wonderful ballet, invention of hope, for despair.

The bright eyes may flicker an instant, and then
For pennies comes a gipsy boy balancing on his toes.
But the animals haven't finished going up and going down
In the panoramic, breathless Noah's Ark merry-go-round.

Angel, hold on. The moon is adrift,
The meridian oscillates visibly. Quick, a theodolite!
Hark, the big guns go off! Look, the pretty fireworks
Making faces at heaps of people on a black heath.

## On One Condition

If there were an open way
   A stairway leading back to those soft-lidded skies
And in the tree-top voices that say
   Shall come, it shall come, for it shall come
   A door half open to surprise
   The dead sun's red baffled in those eyes.
If the writing in the road
   Had led a stranger's foot nearer that door and in
And the flicker of passing people told
   How soon that world shall end, this world shall come
   How soon shall time be tense, and shivering skin
   Out of a touch make the worlds kin.

If appearances, and across
   The appearances the names, their square of sense between,
   Had saved enough to leave to lose
   And gathered up in arms all that shall come
   And the seen and the unseen
   Had stood the one behind the other
If it had been.


## Landscape I

The character of a landscape stands always in a mysterious relation
   to the soul of man.

And while he thought thus and lay on skins on the ground, the
   jaguars swam through the stream, and played round his resting-
   place.

The instruments had to share the couch of the travellers at
   night.

And gave science an insight into the analogy of natural formations,
   and the ruling laws of the globe in reference to its veins of
   water.


## The Birds of Tin

The birds of tin
We cannot eat.

We play with them
They cost us nothing
The birds of tin
Municipal

They fly, they float
They wave to us
From far away
They come to rest
Perfectly flat
    medals
Of innumerable sizes
On the surface of the sea.
Some are enormously large
Some are six feet high
Some you can hold
Some you can put in your mouth
Some slip through your fingers
And there are microscopic
    tiny birds.
In vain we speak to them
In vain we call to them
Or entreat them to open their wings.

# E. L. T. MESENS

born 1903

## The Arid Husband

My adored statue.

The soil ordinarily so hard
And the wing hung from a cry
Miraculously give place
To a soft soil
To a vapid and perpetual song.

I have loved you so much
That my tailor himself
Does not recognise me.

I have wanted you so much
That the lamplighter no longer calls
At our house

I have built you wildly
And without afterthought.

Now that the dial
Marks each hour an hour less,
From advantage to advantage
All more and more is lost.
Jam for you for all
The knapsack

The fieldmarshal without shame
The humming bird without bitterness
The triangle that cannot find a place
The unavowed brute
The moralist without glory.

And believe
My dear statue of paste
In the bankless affection
Of your ultimate spouse
Your true arid husband.

# ROLAND PENROSE

born 1900

Selections from
*The Road is Wider Than Long:*
*An Image Diary from the Balkans, July–August 1938*\*

They breathe with the night
in houses whose marble veins
are washed with sail cloth

whose carpets are covered with olives

whose gardens begin under the sea

they breathe with the night
enemy the S U N closes their eyes
the day of summer lasts
until the earthquake hatches
from the dream of heat
the dream of cold.

Let us through
lift your four striped arms
and let us through

we need dancing
young grass
children to sing for rain

A S K have we got time
we want more than they are
willing to allow

---

\*In its original form Roland Penrose's poem interweaves with photographs
and collages, and appears in red and black type of differing faces. The editor
regrets that publishing costs make facsimile reproduction impossible. In this
edited version, asterisks indicate ellipses in the text.

their wasp helmets their guns
their guns pointing
to the ticket office

have we got time
have we got papers
have we got money
have we got ice

Dragomir Stanescu wants to see you.
He has got the ice with eggs painted
on it, made specially for the peasants.
But he knows that we shall not need
it nor anything else. It will be dark.
We shall not know which is the inn
and which the church – that is the
prison for the Fascists, that the grave-
year for the Communists –

## NO POLITICS HERE

This cart that blocks the road has been
at work for six hundred years
Standing to their necks in water
its men cut reeds
Leeches eat their bones
Their throats are too dry to sing

they have not earned
six days leisure
six days to sing auf tzac
and the road is blocked

*     *     *

HAVE YOU SEEN the woman
age 100 asleep on the sledge

the man who lost a leg in America
and an arm at Bran

the blind man with 3 eyes
the dwarf who can play the flute with his foot

they can all sing
                EVERY JACK MAN
and the little girl
whose breasts begin to break the plain
whose sisters lie clothed in crops
their valleys fertile
their springs sacred

Vapours escape from the rocks
writing tomorrow's news in the sky
we have forgotten yesterday
and tomorrow's news is bad news
our children need medical attention
we need a house without walls
surrounded by fire
the doors open to all who can see

our road is wider than long.

                *     *     *

At Kalkis everybody is in the street
there is no room in the streets
there is no room in the houses
they have come for the earthquake
and they don't understand
                        they smile
they send a pair of eyes with ice
the little girls talk endlessly
holding hands across the road
they clutch at my fingers
there are sixteen children
swinging on my eyelids

They show us the way
to a beach with flying fish and laugh

\*  \*  \*

The Macedonian whose flute kills
stands everywhere
his bears will dance
they forget the dust for a little music
the Macedonian will be able to buy
a pair of good eyes for his bride

That will be after the rain and
after the storm
which makes of the mountains a lake
blinding with red hail
mixing earth fire water and air
in the same pot
hitting across the steppe
on both cheeks
the naked peasant

Until then nothing can be done
we can only talk in whispers in the hotel
the town is sick but no one dare say so
Maritza up behind the North Station
could cure it
her green leaves
the strength of her pigeon voice
heal where other music wounds

each note wounds the last heals

the porters the suburban peasant
the policeman and the minister's wife
all go to her

she gave power to the last dictator
and then killed him with a needle
the gold magnate
whose image is already painted
among the saints
will also die suddenly

Maritza is strong
the porter puts his sou
into the belly of her guitar
her understanding is his security.

Every evening the shops burn
white blocks in bandages receive their guests
a rich organization fetches visitors from the
cellars and spreads them out in groups
tomorrow they will be driven to the next city

\*      \*      \*

Lovers who escape who are free to separate
free to re-unite leave their tongues
plaited together hidden in the dry grass
folded in peasant cloth
embalmed in the green memories of desire

To avoid the danger of not meeting next year
She must tie her hair round the branches
Leave your tongue
Stuck
To the bark

then the journeys alone that fill
the world become fertile
in each tower on each headland
as the frontier is passed
lovers watching for the red train
have grown into each other's eyes

the colour of their hope is
the white feather of a volcano
the blue eyes
which opens in the clouds before sunset
the stage of a greek theatre echoing
the smile that drops from her lips

like bats they make love by day
their heads buried in the stones
their feet searching for lions in the hills.

At night we found a deserted city
water ran under the streets
the houses dry and full of herbs
formed the labyrinth of a dead shell
a boy inside a column was still alive
another 500 years will deliver him
the Americans are the first in the field
with an offer of clothes and a scholarship

\*    \*    \*

Magic lived in this rock
these stones have seen seventeen battles
the Assyrians the Turks and the Australians
landed here
these crops grow in human blood they
are the finest in Europe
the public gardens have the tallest fountains
of any city since Thebes

The
BAND
CONCERT
will
begin

NOW

The cockpit the bull ring the open air
cinema the dance hall the committee
room and the black exchange
are at work
turning their bloodshot melodies

                          while Maritza
tunes the two chords of her guitar.

# PHILIP O'CONNOR

born 1916

*Poems*

### 1

1780 a.d. in the street they flung foam about and a young funny gentleman poured the juices of a ton of blood oranges down upon the people

the iron cockerel on St Dunstan's spun round after hens of the air and worried the frosty smoke with his dark alarums

they rushed down the lane without breaking glass or digging mounds then thundered into the midst of the newly unleashed Sunday Express very red after a long night journey and crowded with gesticulating poetesses

### 2

1066 a.d. the saxon put his foot upon the ground the five women fell upon him but he put his foot upon the ground Norman William put his boats upon the sea to take him to England where he put his foot upon the ground once landed and his multitudinous strong and skilled men shew sufficient to take Britain which they did

### 3

the high man faced the London crowd from the plinth of Nelson's Column wagged his mighty finger at six hundred thousand white faces grouped in a posy of living humanity I am he howled
you are they whispered like the knocking of clouds handsome Nelson swayed in the gale and the cold pigeons rested upon his shoulder

### 4

gravely the assembled chimney-stacks walked into the
high street where the various wombs were displaying
unborn children in Midnight Market

### 5

Captain Busby put his beard in his mouth and sucked it,
then took it out and spat on it then put it in and sucked it
then walked on down the street thinking hard.
Suddenly he put his wedding-ring in his trilby hat and put
the hat on a passing kitten. Then he carefully calculated the
width of the pavement with a pair of adjustable sugar-
tongs. This done he knitted his brows. Then he walked on

thinking hard

### 6

Captain Busted Busby frowned hard at a passing ceiling
and fixed his eye upon a pair of stationary taxies. Suddenly
he went up to one of them and addressed himself to the
driver. He discharged his socks and continued whistling.
The taxi saluted but he put up with it, and puckered a
resigned mouth and knitted a pair of thoughtful eyebrows.

### 7

M. looking out of his window with purple curtains saw
Captain Busby thoughtfully chewing a less impatient por-
tion of his walking-stick unostentatiously against a lamp-
post. The road was blue but Captain Busby seemed a very
dark green with ivory face (for it was night time). He
frowned. He looked up to the top of the rapidly emptying
street. He cut his hair slowly. He looked at the bottom of
the street. He made rapid measurements with a pair of
adjustable sugar-tongs. These he afterwards secreted in

his trousers. He then flew into his friend's apartment
through the willingly opened window.

### 8

Marcella waited for her lover outside a public house known
to both of them. Immediately Captain Busby appeared
holding a woman in his arms. This wasn't true thought
Marcella carefully, and was relieved to see that God had
thrown a lamp-post at the Captain, temporarily disabling
him.

### 9

He arranged himself in sugar and put himself in his bath
and prepared to breathe his last

his four bottles lay grouped around him

do your duty in this world and gather dividends from the dog
thrown at you

goodbye my children

and he died and they huskily nailed down his coffin
and put it in ten feet of sod
and grouped around him reading the will

for indeed and forever would he be
to them
just dad

### 10

Mother lay crying in the withdrawing room
bitterly bewailing cruel fate who with a flick of his pen
had so completely shattered the even tenour of her ways

sobbed upon the brick platform shaking her fist at every
　　porter who passed
declaring cruel fate who with a flick of his pen
had so cruelly broken
the even tenour of her ways


## II

she considered the porter with the cap on the side of his head
　　fitfully
who had squandered his sweet-peas upon her
who had ridden every train and blown all whistles
to feast his evil frontal eyes on her to break the even tenour
　　of her ways

she shunted her back to him
she put on her large black hat with insolent vulgarity
and deliberately smirked into his face
she thrust a carrot into his face
he gravely took it and handed it without moving a muscle of
　　his face
to the dominant personality of the station
the station master himself

events moved indefatigably to their long-awaited climax
the station master seized the carrot and conveyed it to a
　　drawer
reserved for matters of importance
and seizing a document asserting his credentials and authority
motored along the platform and alighted at the lady

madam he said coldly
your carrot is in the drawer
pray come for it or suitable measures will be taken to enforce
the union of yourself and the personality
who broke the even tenour of your ways

lightning juggled above the station portraying its grim
    battlements
thunder crashed upon the assembled people
she threw three flashes of self-possessed rays
at him from her large radiant eyes
she ran to the drawer refusing the automobile
she snatched abruptly at the carrot
scenting with inexorable female intuition the precise position
    afforded it by reason of its pre-eminent significance
she ran from the room like a bitten wounded thing
and fell laughing upon the station master who had broken the
    even
tenour of her ways

he was busy
he was doing his duty
he rattled the cans
he gave out composed answers to the backchat following his
    curt commands
he went on with his duty forgetting
that he had broken the even tenour of her ways

She walked thoughtfully upon a sugar-box
and would there and then have harangued the station officials
    to compel the attention of the porter

but he did not
but he could not
but he did not
and could not should as he had broken the even tenour of her
    ways

## Fag-End

the drips surprise. They talk too
loud about death (the flanged wheel
brimming with steel that chuckles,
flings glittering eyes on the soil
and shakes the very trees).
The drips creep on as statesmen creep on
in the shadow, pawing every obstacle
and peering for goblins while a parliament house
holds her wide arms over and a clock boldly strikes 5
and shrieks rigidly banging the norm and the quiet people;
say to those arms: Turn.
Upon the creased mud, slums,
and the crafty human structures
negotiate the obstreperous train of drips as well
as the great laws, like charging umbrellas
thrusting through the doorway
sprinkled with the radiant names
of our wine-eyed rulers (one who tosses his fringe of hair back
when he drinks his soup on a mellow table).
Sing like a wheel sing from a mad chest
drunken hearty looking at the puddles
over the gangways of smoke from night to slumdom
and twirl your sunshade to hide
your blonde strawed skull from the
white
multitude of drips.

## The Raspberry in the Pudding

The man in the red scarf comes – from five split places
sudden appeared within the flares,
gold lamps and woven songs of tramways. Those songs in his
    head move around
with their one sound's finger here and fingers there, above has
    cleaved with crooked light
the spitting lightning,
as this could be a storm and all.
His pantaloons are flying below eyes like movie-films, so bright
and their lights so changing in interest – very wild, stormy! and
    it is electric,
that twitch of his bright white ear
a curved and wind-moulded drop adaptable as water
to your mound of sounds. Down the steep road with coalshine
    comes
the startling and laughing man of the moment – a cinema door
has perhaps spat him up from where the organ draws rising hills – or
a clinic, fussy and epigrammatic, or an old awful dome
of a large church like Paul's.
Never mind, rising, falling stomach of mother the doomy mind,
thought large and wide and preposterous that years push along
    adding coating
of sleep or comfort. That loud man of the moment
is late or conceited or takes the wrong turning or is quodded for
    not paying his busfare –
be sure as the turning of a very strong wheel
you will not see him come any nearer. He is a sensation,
for newspapers and headaches. He is exploded!

# DJUNA BARNES

born 1892

## *Transfiguration*

The prophet digs with iron hands
Into the shifting desert sands.

The insect back to larva goes;
Struck to seed the climbing rose.

To Moses' empty gorge, like smoke
Rush inward all the words he spoke.

The knife of Cain lifts from the thrust;
Abel rises from the dust.

Pilate cannot find his tongue;
Bare the tree where Judas hung.

Lucifer roars up from earth;
Down falls Christ into his death.

To Adam back the rib is plied,
A creature weeps within his side.

Eden's reach is thick and green;
The forest blows, no beast is seen.

The unchained sun, in raging thirst,
Feeds the last day to the first.

# ROBERT CONQUEST

born 1917

## *The Agents*

His head like a fist rooted in his abdomen;
His lips like a leather loudspeaker, never kissed;
Hatred simmering in his brain-pan; a thin mist
Blowing the sight from his shifting eye. A pen
Of enormous lightning scrabbles a halo around
The muscle-bound solidity of this saint.
All the fluids of his body are irritant.
All its apertures emit prophetic sounds.

Up on the balcony he clangs and glistens
Freezing the worship at a pole of hate,
To serve that blizzard's huge austerities.
But a warmer sound starts softly; crackle and fizz;
Fibres of fear that smoulder in his heart.
It is to this that everybody listens.

# CHAINPOEMS*

### International Chainpoem

When a parasol is cooled in the crystal garden,
one spire radiates and the other turns round;
a toad, the Unwanted, counts the ribs' teardrops
while I mark each idol in its dregs.
There is a shredded voice, there are three fingers
that follow to the end a dancing gesture
and pose a legend under the turning shade
where the girl's waterfall drops its piece.
Then balls of ennui burst one by one,
by and by metallic metres escape from ceramic pipes.
Oh sun, glass of cloud, adrift in the vast sky,
spell me out a sonnet of a steel necklace.

*Authors (by line):* 1. Takesi Fuji 2. Katue Kitasono 3. Charles Henri Ford
4. Dorian Cooke 5. Norman MacCaig 6. Gordon Sylander 7. George M.
O'Donnell 8. Parker Tyler 9. Saburoh Kuroda 10. Nagao Hirao 11. Syuiti
Nagayasu 12. Tuneo Osada

### Lyric by Nine

With the forks of flowers I eat the meat of morning,
then soon am stiff with the salt spew of your swiftest curse;
as your untoward beauty flecks the trembling lip of water,
ripe man, I shall cut you down among the weeds,

* Chainpoems are a variation of the surrealist game 'The Exquisite Corpse'
in which a group of people compose a sentence, each contributing one word
in order without knowing what the others have written. The game was named
after the first sentence so composed: 'The exquisite corpse drinks the red
wine.' Most chainpoems are simply group efforts; each poet contributes a line
after reading what has preceded. Charles Henri Ford speculates that 'The
blueprint of the chainpoem is the anonymous shape lying in a hypothetical
joint imagination, which builds as though the poem were a series of either
mathematical or dream progressions.'

publish the recipe for the sunset on your thighs,
and, ripe man, remove the throat between my shoulder-blades and
   wings.
Now let us change the dawn into a subject for crime:
here is the trout of evening that swam and played with everything
and came alive upon someone that was guiltless!

*Authors (by line):* 1. Charles Henri Ford 2. Forest Anderson 3. Troy Garrison
4. Gordon Sylander 5. Parker Tyler 6. Paul Eaton Reeve 7. Nicolas Calas
8. Napier Towne 9. Hillary Arm


## Dirge for Three Trumpets

Surprising my dupe by his egg of Oedipus
My brow grows horns that whisper like knives
While his hair on bended knee goes gold.
When my sister was raped by the tractor amok
I was standing astride the street of the birds
Molesting the ants whose home was a cloud,
And the endless nudity of a knife ajar
Showed me the chicken-faced heart of a room.
Before my last foot spreads like a plague,
In the eye of transformations a mirror reveals
The lips of my mother: a wound on my ankle.
At the bottom of delirium, the coherent coin
Overturns its shadow, solid, disquieting
As the snake that flies on its one hind leg.
Open the divinatory spots on the moon,
The daily silence of unearthed mysteries!
The skeleton world grows the flesh of blindness,
Purple as tongues the water-lion tears out,
And the infinite sadness of the anus-eyed man
Sings of the wink of the sphinx of the sea.
The cold city falls in drops of hot rain.

*Authors (successive lines):* 1. Matta Echaurren 2. Parker Tyler 3. Charles Henri
Ford

## Anglo-American Chainpoem

The leaf knows sorrow in this time of thorns,
Red-gold the country's treasure cropped by sword,
A gale of bristles blown across the land.
On days when playing for safety spits out blood and stone,
And evenings when white revolver, exhalation of the trees,
Smokes mist across the mouth, men take the signposts down,
Frozen to the north of the time-cropped town.

Sucking the berry's map, they curse the fired seed
No noose can amnesty nor eyelid truncheon,
For they have crossed their rubicons of blood.
The terrible thunder crushes autumn's insects!
The twisting eyes on the stalks of rue and reed
Show Europe's laugh! Europe's pearl rope of death
Her kings dangle to the masses from imperial fingers.

*Authors (by line):* 1. J. F. Hendry 2. Conroy Maddox 3. Robert Melville
4. Nicholas Moore 5. John Bayliss 6. Mary Woodman 7. Henry Treece
8. Parker Tyler 9. John Hastings 10. Troy Garrison 11. H. R. Hays 12. Robert
Friend 13. Harry Roskolenko 14. Elgar Houghton

# DYLAN THOMAS

1914–1953

## January 1939

Because the pleasure-bird whistles after the hot wires,
Shall the blind horse sing sweeter?
Convenient bird and beast lie lodged to suffer
The supper and knives of a mood.
In the sniffed and poured snow on the tip of the tongue of the year
That clouts the spittle like bubbles with broken rooms,
An enamoured man alone by the twigs of his eyes, two fires,
Camped in the drug-white shower of nerves and food,
Savours the lick of the times through a deadly wood of hair
In a wind that plucked a goose,
Nor ever, as the wild tongue breaks its tombs,
Rounds to look at the red, wagged root.
Because there stands, one story out of the bum city,
That frozen wife whose juices drift like a fixed sea
Secretly in statuary,
Shall I, struck on the hot and rocking street,
Not spin to stare at an old year
Toppling and burning in the muddle of towers and galleries
Like the mauled pictures of boys?
The salt person and blasted place
I furnish with the meat of a fable.
If the dead starve, their stomachs turn to tumble
An upright man in the antipodes
Or spray-based and rock-chested sea:
Over the past table I repeat this present grace.

## I, in My Intricate Image

### I

I, in my intricate image, stride on two levels,
Forged in man's minerals, the brassy orator
Laying my ghost in metal,
The scales of this twin world tread on the double,
My half ghost in armour hold hard in death's corridor,
To my man-iron sidle.

Beginning with doom in the bulb, the spring unravels,
Bright as her spinning-wheels, the colic season
Worked on a world of petals;
She threads off the sap and needles, blood and bubble
Casts to the pine roots, raising man like a mountain
Out of the naked entrail.

Beginning with doom in the ghost, and the springing marvels,
Image of images, my metal phantom
Forcing forth through the harebell,
My man of leaves and the bronze root, mortal, unmortal,
I, in my fusion of rose and male motion,
Create this twin miracle.

This is the fortune of manhood: the natural peril,
A steeplejack tower, bonerailed and masterless,
No death more natural;
Thus the shadowless man or ox, and the pictured devil,
In seizure of silence commit the dead nuisance:
The natural parallel.

My images stalk the trees and the slant sap's tunnel,
No tread more perilous, the green steps and spire
Mount on man's footfall,
I with the wooden insect in the tree of nettles,
In the glass bed of grapes with snail and flower,
Hearing the weather fall.

Intricate manhood of ending, the invalid rivals,
Voyaging clockwise off the symboled harbour,
Finding the water final,
On the consumptives' terrace taking their two farewells,
Sail on the level, the departing adventure,
To the sea-blown arrival.

## II

They climb the country pinnacle,
Twelve winds encounter by the white host at pasture,
Corner the mounted meadows in the hill corral;
They see the squirrel stumble,
The haring snail go giddily round the flower,
A quarrel of weathers and trees in the windy spiral.

As they dive, the dust settles,
The cadaverous gravels, falls thick and steadily,
The highroad of water where the seabear and mackerel
Turn the long sea arterial
Turning a petrol face blind to the enemy
Turning the riderless dead by the channel wall.

(Death instrumental,
Splitting the long eye open, and the spiral turnkey,
Your corkscrew grave centred in navel and nipple,
The neck of the nostril,
Under the mask and the ether, they making bloody
The tray of knives, the antiseptic funeral;

Bring out the black patrol,
Your monstrous officers and the decaying army,
The sexton sentinel, garrisoned under thistles,
A cock-on-a-dunghill
Crowing to Lazarus the morning is vanity,
Dust be your saviour under the conjured soil.)

As they drown, the chime travels,
Sweetly the diver's bell in the steeple of spindrift
Rings out the Dead Sea scale;
And, clapped in water till the triton dangles,
Strung by the flaxen whale-weed, from the hangman's raft,
Hear they the salt glass breakers and the tongues of burial.

(Turn the sea-spindle lateral,
The grooved land rotating, that the stylus of lightning
Dazzle this face of voices on the moon-turned table,
Let the wax disk babble
Shames and the damp dishonours, the relic scraping.
These are your years' recorders. The circular world stands still.)

### III

They suffer the undead water where the turtle nibbles,
Come unto sea-stuck towers, at the fibre scaling,
The flight of the carnal skull
And the cell-stepped thimble;
Suffer, my topsy-turvies, that a double angel
Sprout from the stony lockers like a tree on Aran.

Be by your one ghost pierced, his pointed ferrule,
Brass and the bodiless image, on a stick of folly
Star-set at Jacob's angle,
Smoke hill and hophead's valley,
And the five-fathomed Hamlet on his father's coral,
Thrusting the tom-thumb vision up the iron mile.

Suffer the slash of vision by the fin-green stubble,
Be by the ships' sea broken at the manstring anchored
The stoved bones' voyage downward
In the shipwreck of muscle;
Give over, lovers, locking, and the seawax struggle,
Love like a mist or fire through the bed of eels.

And in the pincers of the boiling circle,
The sea and instrument, nicked in the locks of time,
My great blood's iron single
In the pouring town,
I, in a wind on fire, from green Adam's cradle,
No man more magical, clawed out the crocodile.

Man was the scales, the death birds on enamel,
Tail, Nile, and snout, a saddler of the rushes,
Time in the hourless houses
Shaking the sea-hatched skull,
And, as for oils and ointments on the flying grail,
All-hollowed man wept for his white apparel.

Man was Cadaver's masker, the harnessing mantle,
Windily master of man was the rotten fathom,
My ghost in his metal neptune
Forged in man's mineral.
This was the god of beginning in the intricate seawhirl,
And my images roared and rose on heaven's hill.

# HENRY TREECE

1911–1966

## Horror

Like the fey goose-girl in the enchanted wood,
Whose cloth-of-gold hair curtained her swart sin
So that the feckless linnets stricken by her flute
For homage' sake forgot the bodkin bright,
And so lay waxen in among the moss
About her feet.

Like the gold boy, the weeping pauper prince
Prisoned in a tower of tongues and eyes,
Stumbling from floor to dusty screaming floor,
Upstairs and down stone stairs, whose flaking edge
Is brown with brother's blood. And brother's song
Shrill in his ears.

Like the old traveller, who knew this stormy road
Even before the raven sowed its elms,
Who comes by night upon a lighted house
Where no house was in any other year,
And stops, aghast, to see his own shade propped
Stiff at the board.

## The Magic Wood

*The wood is full of shining eyes,*
*The wood is full of creeping feet,*
*The wood is full of tiny cries:*
*You must not go to the wood at night!*

I met a man with eyes of glass
And a finger as curled as the wriggling worm,
And hair all red with rotting leaves,
And a stick that hissed like a summer snake.

*The wood is full of shining eyes,*
*The wood is full of creeping feet,*
*The wood is full of tiny cries:*
*You must not go to the wood at night!*

He sang me a song in backwards words,
And drew me a dragon in the air.
I saw his teeth through the back of his head,
And a rat's eyes winking from his hair.

*The wood is full of shining eyes,*
*The wood is full of creeping feet,*
*The wood is full of tiny cries:*
*You must not go to the wood at night!*

He made me a penny out of a stone,
And showed me the way to catch a lark
With a straw and a nut and a whispered word
And a pennorth of ginger wrapped up in a leaf.

*The wood is full of shining eyes,*
*The wood is full of creeping feet,*
*The wood is full of tiny cries:*
*You must not go to the wood at night!*

He asked me my name, and where I lived;
I told him a name from my Book of Tales;
He asked me to come with him into the wood
And dance with the Kings from under the hills.

*The wood is full of shining eyes,*
*The wood is full of creeping feet,*
*The wood is full of tiny cries:*
*You must not go to the wood at night!*

But I saw that his eyes were turning to fire;
I watched the nails grow on his wriggling hand;
And I said my prayers, all out in a rush,
And found myself safe on my father's land.

*Oh, the wood is full of shining eyes,*
*The wood is full of creeping feet,*
*The wood is full of tiny cries:*
*You must not go to the wood at night!*

# NICHOLAS MOORE

born 1918

### The Island and the Cattle

Because he sent a head of cattle on
Further than they should go, over the dykes,
Driving them with a switch and a dog beside him:

They sank in the quag, and he,
Frightened because of his sin, disappeared,
Never to be noticed again in that country:

Because he told them, in a letter,
That it was not his fault, he had gone mad,
Driven towards the sea by a vision of birds

Who whistled over his head in the wind,
Leading to a quiet island. He found a girl there,
Lay with her in the rushes, her beauty

Like a star being too much for him.
The wind rose, the morning was grey, his vision gone:
There was no girl, there were no cattle, and it was day.

### Song

A little onion lay by the fireplace,
It had a burning mansion painted on one side,
On the other it had a rat and a pair of whiskers.
I said, My love, this reminds me of you,
But she put out the candle and said, Go to bed.
I cannot remember, said the madman.

The mouse on the floor and the bat on the ceiling
Batten on my memory, O make my bed soon,
Before I see her again, or before the doctor shoots me,
Or the white nurse straps me to my bed like mother.
The midnight lady has lost her echo.
I only remember the onion, the egg, and the boy.
O that was me, said the madman.

### The Patient

The doctor asked him if he dreamed at night,
Did he talk to himself, or others at times,
Not knowing what he said? Did he feel light,
As though he were a pillow. In his dreams,

If he had dreams (he later said he had)
Did he see people that he knew, do things
He really wanted to, but thought were bad?
Or did he make up new imaginings,

Have new sensations, act as if he were
In some strange land, a guest or traveller
Among a different people? Was his world at night
The world he knew in daytime? Did he know
At all what were the thoughts that plagued him so?
I can't remember, he said, but I'm all right.

# JOHN BAYLISS

born 1919

## Seven Dreams

Breaking through the first door, he found
a still lake, luminous by the sallow moon,
burnished with green fire along its banks,
and heard a dry wind beating the bulrush stems,
and there were dead birds in this dream.

But in the next he was a great emperor,
a winged moth over white water,
dizzy with love of the moon's reflection,
and entered to restore the green
emerald under the moonstone lying,
pierced the dark layer but could not breathe –
his lovely wings folding and fading . . .

And later he slept one night lapped in water,
Moses in darkness, as quiet as sleeping moorhen
soft in the shadow by the still shore.

And again he moved with four horsemen
over the stone bridge, the stream leading
into the lake, and left them,
going to gather them water,
seeing a grey swan like a cloud gliding,
and by now he had reached the fifth door.

Which opened on to a brown arcade of fruits
– apricot and mulberry, nectarine, peach,
grape and gold orange by the singing tree,
and there peacocks walked by the fountains
pecking the bright fruit disdainfully,
and he saw the green lake against tall mountains.

But the sixth door led into a dark tower,
a spider had obscured the names on the wall
and water drawn moss across them,
and a black knight stood in the hall,
and against the stairs the echoes rang
as if they were following him,
and the top of the tower shook like a mast,
and the lake was covered by a black mist.

And the last door was without a key
but it lay open to the touch of fingers,
showing the choir of a church,
but he found no singers:
and here lay the fruit like wax
offerings to the red moon,
and he saw the four horsemen
engraved on a grey tomb;
and, glowing in stained glass,
the several peacocks stood
admiring themselves in swan's blood,
and he saw the moth dying
in the fading tree, and the black knight beneath
awaiting its last breath;
then a black bat flying disturbed him
and he thought with dismay of the eighth dream
seeing the lake through the small doorway ...


### Apocalypse and Resurrection

I have seen the white horsemen riding to hell
with their legions fast as light, fierce and inevitable
as volcanic lava, molten frost, invincible
as the great stone that falls from a hill:

and the Cenotaph is breaking in Whitehall
under the artillery of the dead,

and in a thousand parks the grimed memorials
sway in the wind of the counted battalions they record
and the names march into the Council chamber
into the home, the betrayer's bed,
and the mayor is strangled with his scarlet cord.

And the politician with his great house of promises
runs screaming out of the falling cards,
and the bishop is choked with his warring words:
and the skeleton walks into the brothel
demanding his due and paying the price with a gold
ring that is green from lying long in the earth:
and the great towers topple and crack
as the flat shadows of birds fight
over the crushed flesh, and the white
flash of the moon between clouds
betrays the cold eye watching, the old
inimical star that has driven men mad.

But before they come, there is a dry rustle of leaves
and the wind turns a little from the hill,
and hands come out of the tombs in Chiswick Churchyard
and slip into the hands of passers-by,
and all the drugs of cassia and nard
are insufficient to stop the Egyptian mummy
walking out of the British Museum into the Strand.

And in Chiswick House the madmen are throwing their clocks
into the lake, and the wild clack of the geese
echoes the wheels of black coaches drawn up on the gravel:
and dark flowers are breaking the concrete roads of Kew,
and the bridge is burning above the ebony river
in an arc of fire: and the terrace to Richmond Park
is covered with silk and lace and satin and red,
and blue and green and silver dresses that preen
and flutter and pause as they did the day they died
and the dress was laid in the press and the wearer laid
in the marble vault smoothing her last brocade.

On these, on us, on the dust of centuries,
the image of glass, or gilt or porcelain,
the moving figures of Madame Tussaud's that walked
only at night, now walking their last domain,
– on these the white wind rustled, the raving horse
reared to the sky and fell like a fountain of ice
covering all: the stone and the dark remain
sole effigies of all the creatures that ran
or fought, or dreamed throughout the dissident years
and the white horsemen who passed have ended their wars.

# KENNETH PATCHEN

1911–1972

## The Naked Land

A beast stands at my eye.

I cook my senses in a dark fire.
The old wombs rot and the new mother
Approaches with the footsteps of a world.

Who are the people of this unscaled heaven?
*What beckons?*
Whose blood hallows this grim land?
What slithers along the watershed of my human sleep?

The other side of knowing . . .
Caress of unwaking delight . . . O start
A sufficient love! O gently silent forms
Of the last spaces.


## 'In the footsteps of the walking air'

In the footsteps of the walking air
Sky's prophetic chickens weave their cloth of awe
And hillsides lift green wings in somber journeying.

Night in his soft haste bumps on the shoulders of the abyss
And a single drop of dark blood covers the earth.

Now is the China of the spirit at walking
In my reaches.
A sable organ sounds in my gathered will
And love's inscrutable skeleton sings.

My seeing moves under a vegetable shroud
And dead forests stand where once Mary stood.

Sullen stone dogs wait in the groves of water ...
– Though the wanderer drown, his welfare is as a fire
That burns at the bottom of the sea, warming
Unknown roads for sleep to walk upon.

### A Temple

To leave the earth was my wish, and no will stayed my rising.
Early, before sun had filled the roads with carts
Conveying folk to weddings and to murders;
Before men left their selves of sleep, to wander
In the dark of the world like whipped beasts.

I took no pack. I had no horse, no staff, no gun.
I got up a little way and something called me,
Saying,
'Put your hand in mine. We will seek God together.'
And I answered,
'It is your father who is lost, not mine.'
Then the sky filled with tears of blood, and snakes sang.

### Saturday Night in the Parthenon

Tiny green birds skate over the surface of the room.
A naked girl prepares a basin with steaming water,
And in the corner away from the hearth, the red wheels
Of an up-ended chariot slowly turn.
After a long moment, the door to the other world opens
And the golden figure of a man appears. He stands
Ruddy as a salmon beside the niche where are kept

The keepsakes of the Prince of Earth; then sadly, drawing
A hammer out of his side, he advances to an oaken desk,
And being careful to strike in exact fury, pounds it to bits.
Another woman has by now taken her station
Beside the bubbling tub.
Her legs are covered with a silken blue fur,
Which in places above the knees
Grows to the thickness of a lion's mane.
The upper sphere of her chest
Is gathered into huge creases by two jeweled pins.
Transparent little boots reveal toes
Which an angel could want.
Beneath her on the floor a beautiful cinnamon cat
Plays with a bunch of yellow grapes, running
Its paws in and out like a boy being a silly king.
Her voice is round and white as she says:
'Your bath is ready, darling. Don't wait too long.'
But he has already drawn away to the window
And through its circular opening looks,
As a man into the pages of his death.
'Terrible horsemen are setting fire to the earth.
Houses are burning . . . the people fly before
The red spears of a speckled madness . . .'
'Please, dear,' interrupts the original woman,
'We cannot help them . . . Under the cancerous foot
Of their hatred, they were born to perish –
Like beasts in a well of spiders . . .
Come now, sweet; the water will get cold.'
A little wagon pulled by foxes lowers from the ceiling.
Three men are seated on its cushions which breathe
Like purple breasts. The head of one is tipped
To the right, where on a bed of snails, a radiant child
Is crowing sleepily; the heads of the other two are turned
Upward, as though in contemplation
Of an authority which is not easily apprehended.
Yet they act as one, lifting the baby from its rosy perch,
And depositing it gently in the tub.
The water hisses over its scream . . . a faint smell

Of horror floats up. Then the three withdraw
With their hapless burden, and the tinny bark
Of the foxes dies on the air.
'It hasn't grown cold yet,' the golden figure says,
And he strokes the belly of the second woman,
Running his hands over her fur like someone asleep.
They lie together under the shadow of a giant crab
Which polishes its thousand vises beside the fire.
Farther back, nearly obscured by kettles and chairs,
A second landscape can be seen; then a third, fourth,
Fifth . . . until the whole, fluted like a rose,
And webbed in a miraculous workmanship,
Ascends unto the seven thrones
Where Tomorrow sits.
Slowly advancing down these shifting levels,
The white Queen of Heaven approaches.
Stars glitter in her hair. A tree grows
Out of her side, and gazing through the foliage
The eyes of the Beautiful gleam – 'Hurry, darling,'
The first woman calls. 'The water is getting cold.'
But he does not hear.
The hilt of the knife is carved like a scepter
And like a scepter gently sways
Above his mutilated throat . . .
Smiling like a fashionable hat, the furry girl
Walks quickly to the tub, and throwing off
Her stained gown, eels into the water.
The other watches her sorrowfully; then,
Without haste, as one would strangle an owl,
She flicks the wheel of the chariot – around
Which the black world bends . . .
    without thrones or gates, without faith,
    warmth or light for any of its creatures;
    where even the children go mad – and
As though unwound on a scroll, the picture
Of Everyman's murder winks back at God.

Farther away now, nearly hidden by the human,
Another landscape can be seen . . .
And the wan, smiling Queen of Heaven appears
For a moment on the balconies of my chosen sleep.

# CHARLES HENRI FORD

born 1913

## Plaint

*Before a Mob of 10,000 at Owensboro, Ky.*

I, Rainey Betha, 22,
from the top-branch of race-hatred look at you.
My limbs are bound, though boundless the bright sun
like my bright blood which had to run
into the orchard that excluded me:
now I climb death's tree.

The pruning-hooks of many mouths
cut the black-leaved boughs.
The robins of my eyes hover where
sixteen leaves fall that were a prayer:
sixteen mouths are open wide;
the minutes like black cherries
drop from my shady side.

*Oh, who is the forester must tend such a tree, Lord?*
*Do angels pick the cherry-blood of folk like me, Lord?*


## Somebody's Gone

There may be a basement to the Atlantic
but there's no top-storey
to my mountain of missing you.

I must say your deportment took a hunk
out of my peach of a heart.
I ain't insured against torpedoes!
My turpentine tears would fill a drugstore.

May I be blindfolded before you come my way again
if you're going to leave dry land like an amphibian;
I took you for some kind of ambrosial bird
with no thought of acoustics.

Maybe it's too late to blindfold me ever:
I'm just a blotter crisscrossed with the ink
of words that remind me of you.

Bareheaded aircastle,
you were as beautiful as a broom made of flesh and hair.

When you first disappeared
I couldn't keep up with my breakneck grief,
and now I know how grief can run away with the mind,
leaving the body desolate as a staircase.

## The Overturned Lake

Blue unsolid tongue, if you could talk,
the mountain would supply the brain;
but mountains are mummies: the autobus and train,
manmade worms, disturb their centuries.
Tongue of a deafmute, the lake
shudders, inarticulate.

You are like the mind of a man, too:
surface reflecting the blue day,
the life about you seemingly organized, revolving about you,
you as a center,
but I am concerned in your overthrow:
I should like to pick you up, as if you were a woman of water,
hold you against the light and see your veins flow
with fishes; reveal the animal-flowers that rise
nightlike beneath your eyes.

Noiseless as memory, blind as fear,
lake, I shall make you into a poem,
for I would have you unpredictable as the human body:
I shall equip you with the strength of a dream,
rout you from your blue unconscious bed,
overturn your unconcern,
as the mind is overturned by memory, the heart by dread.


### The Bad Habit

#### (For Poe)

Drug of the incomprehensible
engenders the freaks of desire.
The bleeding statue, the violin's hair,
the river of fire:

the blood grows, the hair flows, the river groans,
from the veins, from the skin, by the home of the child
pulled and repelled by Bloody Bones;
renewal of the swoon

mastered, the raw egg of fear,
doped with mystery, the hooded heart:
perpetually haunted, hopeless addict,
herding unheard of cattle!

Rider on the bat-winged horse.


### 'January wraps up the wound of his arm'

January wraps up the wound of his arm,
January, thieving as a boy, hides the jewel,
sunset, bright bleeding equation.

Day has written itself out, a giveaway, a poem
that balks like a horse before the ditch of night.

Tomorrow, the gash will be an eye:
a drop of dew will travel up his cheek,
like a tear that has changed its mind.

## There's No Place to Sleep in This Bed, Tanguy

The storks like elbows had a fit of falling
She beat me over the head with a lung
Somewhere a voice is calling Picasso
And the lasso of love has the ghost of a chance

The bewildering pathos of a bag of china candy
The hole in the rock where the sea lost hope
The faceless spectators whose tears have no shadows
Ah for this and these my poems are undone

There's no place to sleep in this bed, Tanguy
The wires are cut that connect us with slumber
And the number of day and the number of night is one!
Those grains of sand are menacing as statues

Fountains of fire await the painted trigger
And the nails you drove in the earth have sprung up
Madonnas and torture-machines tell the time
You touch a cloud the rain becomes an object

Whose bow is the rainbow whose arrow is Egypt
Whose target unknown whose quarry is fear
For these are skeletons we never saw before
With skin like candies and no tongue to toss on

You've set new traps for ancient dreams
Oh tame them and train them before they get caught!
There's no place to sleep in this bed, Tanguy
There are too many monuments of broken hearts

# SABUROH KURODA

### *Afternoon 3*

Countless things escape easily out of me,
As if a breeze blows through fingers.
There were some floatages,
Having settled on the sand
After drift.
I pick up a broken piece of pencil.
I drop a broken piece of pencil.
In the dry air, quietly,
My head burns, my hair burns.
Lao-tsze!
What is more inflammable than head or hair?
As long as man does not move,
The horizon
Means to be blind.
Solitude, which reminds me of an old woman,
Eating a peanut, alone in the dead of night,
Runs at full speed on a white bicycle,
Scattering a handful of ashes.
A crab shows its face out of the pit.
A crab puts its face into the pit.

# THOMAS MERTON

1915–1968

## Lent in a Year of War

One of you is a major made of cord and catskin,

And never dreams his eyes may come to life, and thread
The needle-light of famine in a waterglass.

One of you is the paper Jack of Sprites
And will not cast his sentinel voice
Spiralling up the dark ears of the wind,
Where the prisoner's yell is lost.

'What if it was our thumbs put out the sun
When the lance and cross made their mistake?
You'll never rob us our Eden of drumskin shelters,
You, with the bite of John the Baptist's halter,
Getting away in the basket of Paul,
Loving the answer of death, the mother of Lent!'

Thus, in the evening of their sinless murders,
Jack and the major, tossing the coin for a sign,
See the north-south horizon parting like a string.

# NORMAN MacCAIG

born 1910

### Betweens

To hear a dripping water tap in a house
That has no tap in it, in the dead of night.
To hear footsteps come naturally to the door
And stop there forever. In bed in an empty room
To hear a voice on the pillow say *Hello*.

A wheatstalk dances lasciviously in the fire.
My hand drags its plough across this white field.
My head from a sort of radiance watches a chair
Continually completing its meaning. A picture
Tries to plunge from its nail to the centre of the earth.

Immense tides wash through everything. My knuckles
Are tiny whirlpools in it. I stream sideways.
The room's roots are straining. Sounds of the fire
Unmuffle themselves from black coal, are a theatre.
My foot rocks because my heart says so.

How could things stop? And three plump cheers for distance …
To shake a hand and be left with it. To see
Sight cramming itself into an eye and wheat
A harrow of fire: and all a correspondence
Shielding the truth and giving birth to it.

## Poem

There is a wailing baby under every stone and you walk
like a gallant ship three times round the tide.
You wail in the sea's centre and lure sandspits
round a fishing-boat and with chalk
fingers you scribble silly dreams on the sides
of breakwaters and bathers. The red and green caps

of lichen fold gently down to soothe the baby mouths
and the sea rocks the moon in her arms
and the sailors swing to the rowing song of the fishing-boat.
But still tears smoke upwards and foam
is a lightning of sorrow and other earths
rock this one, so queerly stuck in the sun's throat.

# ROBERT HORAN

born 1922

## *By Hallucination Visited*

Come inside the weather
where the wind ended, pulling
the ropes of birds. They flew
in winter disorder and boned their eyes
against the thunder.

And the bright, belled cloud
swung under the odor of lightning;
struck each rock, foot, tree, eye,
each inch of that blood-budded heaven
out of its once gold haven, to blanch
and widen, to knuckle in knotted rain,
to fall and roll in the hands of wood
and water like a silver grain.

Animals, enormous in the telescope of weather
trampled the damp eggs. Leaves were piled
into pimpled houses, and the stained beasts
hid their heads like gelatin in caves.

*

By such a token we emptied the basements
of silk, and beat the rats with sticks
and let the river overrun them.
By such an omen we opened the windows
and bled the rooms, and filled the closets
with hands of mercury. By this knowledge
of weather we spaded our bodies, and planted
the damp statues of wool in the road of the tongue.

*

He could listen, could unlock the water
and watch the stitched salmon lip their swinging
prison; could walk that winter with hands in waves.
And the levels of rain would confuse him,
or he would be reminded thereof.

# SANDERS RUSSELL

### *Poem*

I keep feeling all space as my image
but lines are leading beyond the image
and what they touch is the marvelous.
A green and a red dragon climb mating from the design;
an injured ball keeps fluttering toward the opening;
it can never quite make the ascent.
As if brought home by the touch of fur
the surface opposite is the one I love
as bare as a geography.
At the top of the map a bird is crying;
in the middle a flower is stuck in water;
an apple shines held aloft against a nebula.
Three objects knock together under my dream;
three elements of recognition become new numbers.

# RANDALL JARRELL

1914–1965

## The Islands

Man, if I said once, 'I know,'
Laugh at me, stuff in my angry mouth
Your rueful and foolish laughter. Man is a stone.

Lips own love; did I say once, 'I love'?
I said a word. When the hands told they were love,
I bled and I was beautiful. Man is a knife.

When I said blood, I say I bled.
Is man no more than pain? Speak for me, scars.
Knife holds for me no blood but mine –

When I told I could wish for more than you,
Death, I was dreaming I had died.
Next year's skull perplexed me like a kiss,

I felt my veins contorted with the tongue
That ran through them like my world's crazy will;
My breath cracks into sleep, time eats my fat,

Friends fall and my mouths fail, I brim to death
– Man's hands were wishes, all my wives were iron,
Death shades me like a sword, and I am kissing –

I sweat to my sea like a floe; blue, blue
Were all the islands of my sleep, I wake, I see –
I saw as I lay dying that unbroken sea.

# TONI DEL RENZIO

### Can You Change a Shilling?

Who dares to drop the pin destruction of our silence
Who intrudes his shadow across our parallel paths
Who throws his paper wrappings in the wind at our faces
Who is this travel-stained person

Who do you ask these questions
Who do you resent him in the landscape

That man is the image of my father

But you are the image of your father
That man is but your reflection in the clouds of dust
Do you dislike your own image

There is a scratched future
   a pattern of sand and shrubs
   a cracked terracotta figurine
   a dirty reproduction of the Gioconda
   a bad snapshot of your breast (out of focus)
   an antique hat on a chromium stand
   a book of poems by a negro lawyer
   a broken gramophone surrounded by the remnants of a feast
      and three corpses
   a sewing machine and a sleeping baby
   a glass bowl full of bloodstained water in which some little fish
      are dying
   a page of typing torn into twentythree pieces
   a rusty sword in a bejewelled scabbard
   a sore of a filthy disease in snow-white bandages

Show me the course you've plotted
Point me the star that guides us
give me the key to the purser's safe

You know the route
The heavens are in your ear
The purser's key fits all the locks
You have the purser's key already
Else how could you penetrate so far

I am the key to all my problems
I am the lord of my desires
I am the prince of pleasures
I am the hunting hound that is chased by the hare
I am the erected tower of instinct
I am the locomotive belching steam and smoke
I am the shadow long at noon and gone by night

Do you know the man who sells dirty postcards
Have you seen the sights of this city
Have you climbed the saint's steps
Will you come to me at midnight

# GEORGE ANTHONY

### *Autumn Evening*

It was the wind
reciting prayers;
up the street we ran
from the limping ghost.

The windows were fountains of hair
when the street curled down with a sigh
waiting the discoveries
of barefoot delicacies.

The windows were dripping with hair
and eyes crawled down those spider stairs
like widows of regret.
It was the wind shook down regret.

The street lay in the ground
as formaldehydes of elsewhere.
A naked dog groped up the livid gutter
under a peeled pear of light.

Hand in hand we ran
through houses of fog.
It was remorse that spliced her hair
to my tobacco beard.

We dared to break the wishbone
before the wish was known.
Down the great river of Now
the silence came like rain.

It was the wind
shook down the eyelids.
The evening fell away to where
a child could sleep.

The street unrolls to yesterday
remembering love
the wistful hands now finding
breasts under cobwebs.

It is the wind returns
to fog the wishing glass.
Your window is a good looking glass.
Why do you wipe your face away?

# WELDON KEES

## 1914–1955

### The Conversation in the Drawingroom

– That spot of blood on the drawingroom wall,
No larger than a thumbnail when I looked a moment ago,
Is spreading, Cousin Agatha, and growing brighter.

Nonsense. The oriole warbles in the sunlight.
The fountains gush luxuriantly above the pool.
The weather is ideal: on the paths a sheen
Of summer provides a constant delight.
I am thinking of affiliating with a new theosophist group.

– Once you could hide it with a nickel.
Now it strangely assumes the shape and size of a palm,
And puts out fingers, Cousin Agatha. Look, examine it!

Some aberration of the wallpaper, no doubt.
Did you have an omelette for lunch, and asparagus?
Mrs Pisgah's husband spoke from the beyond during the seance
Last night at Madame Irani's. He seemed to have a cold.
The tambourine did not function with its usual zest.

– And a wrist, Cousin Agatha, and an arm!
Like those maps in a cinema that spread
Like wind blowing over a field of wheat, Cousin Agatha!

I have warned you, Hobart, about reading 'The Turn of the Screw'
And that story of Balzac's, whatever the name of it is,
Just before retiring. They always have a decidedly bad effect upon
    you.
I believe I will put another aspirin in the lily's vase.
And now I must go to take my nap in the sunroom.

– Cousin Agatha, it moves like a fish, wet,
Wet like a fish, becomes a moving thing
That spreads and reaches from the wall!

I cannot listen to you any more just now, Hobart.
Kindly speak to Marie about the placecards for this evening.
Ah, there is the oriole again; how beautiful the view
From this window! – Yet why, one wonders, must Hobart begin
Gasping and screaming in such a deplorable fashion
There in the drawingroom? It is scarcely considerate.
Youthful animal spirits, one supposes, combined
With a decided taste for the macabre. Where is the barbital?
Marie can never learn to leave it here, by the incense-burner.
Ah, now he has stopped and only thrashes about, rather feebly, on
    the floor.
It is a beautiful afternoon; I will get up about three-fifteen.
Everything is blissfully quiet now. I am ready for sleep.


## The Heat in the Room

A good night for the fireplace to be
Crackling with flames – or so he figured,
Crumpling the papers he could only see
As testimonials to long plateaus of emptiness.

Watching in silence, she tried listening to the storm,
And thought obscurely, 'He is burning both of us.
He is burning up our lives.' She would have gone
To him and touched his hand, except for fear.

The ragged trees in lightning, blacker than before,
Moved nearer to the room. 'If only I could stop
The pounding of my heart,' she thought, 'I might –'
But his face, a tight orange mask that burned,

Was held as though he faced a looking glass
And saw another face behind his own.
The fire seemed about to die. Then suddenly the flames
Roared like a white-hot furnace, and she screamed.

# PART II

*The Second World War to the Present*

# HOWARD SERGEANT

born 1914

## *Man Meeting Himself*

They are moving inwards; the circle is closing.
Tonight I have heard them again among
the houses, a million voices rising as one
in the darkness, hounding our lives with their
pitiless tongues, the voices of leaves and children
crying, as children cry, for light – where is
no light; for love, where there is only silence:

and under my feet stars like dead leaves falling
under my feet the bloodless faces staring . . .

There is one hand, five-barbed with innocence,
can start a conflagration in the breast.
There is one force can find a man his likeness
in a stone, and we have buried it with lies;
but not for ever – we have not earth enough
nor words to turn the wind back from our hearts.
Come day the rocks will open and ourselves
walk out in freedom to startle the world as men.

Look into their eyes and faces if you dare
and, if you dare, describe a victory.
Not history, not hate, flows over them.

And this is guilt –
man meeting himself in the night,
and hating himself and the wind
and the lips of the wind; the swivelling
eye and the lies most known
by the light, the beast in the man
and the man in the beast and himself;

but hating most deeply and deadly
his hatred of self –
to answer
*I do not know their language!*


## The Inundation

Moon at the full. Europe has burst its banks
and the first floodwaters rising reach our doors.
Look down, you lovers, now, from your high towers;
your stone cannot long withstand their violent fingers
*who were no enemies*

And you who kept the willows bright by summer
or by winter conjured aprils from the flesh,
look to your trophies now – desire is withered
at their cold breath, the born and the unborn riding
*who were no enemies*

And you who dreamt of islands winking in the sun,
horizons like stepping-stones beneath your heels,
but feared too much the faring – they know well
your shallow harbours, the dead and the half-dead rising
*who were no enemies*

Soldiers and civilians, all you who shouted
in the streets, first for a saviour, but louder
for the killer, your catchwords will not appease
them now, the dispossessing and the dispossessed
*who were no enemies*

Not even you whose hands were clean, the mass-
observers perched upon the skull-shaped hill,
can hold them with all your monumental tears:
the graves are open and they have taken the cities
*who were no enemies*

# FRANK O'HARA

1926–1966

## Poem

The eager note on my door said 'Call me,
call when you get in!' so I quickly threw
a few tangerines into my overnight bag,
straightened my eyelids and shoulders, and

headed straight for the door. It was autumn
by the time I got around the corner, oh all
unwilling to be either pertinent or bemused, but
the leaves were brighter than grass on the sidewalk!

Funny, I thought, that the lights are on this late
and the hall door open; still up at this hour, a
champion jai-alai player like himself? Oh fie!
for shame! What a host, so zealous! And he was

there in the hall, flat on a sheet of blood that
ran down the stairs. I did appreciate it. There are few
hosts who so thoroughly prepare to greet a guest
only casually invited, and that several months ago.

## Blocks

I

Yippee! she is shooting in the harbor! he is jumping
up to the maelstrom! she is leaning over the giant's
cart of tears which like a lava cone let fall to fly
from the cross-eyed tantrum-tousled ninth grader's
splayed fist is freezing on the cement! he is throwing
up his arms in heavenly desperation, spacious Y of his

tumultuous love-nerves flailing like a poinsettia in
its own nailish storm against the glass door of the
cumulus which is withholding her from these divine
pastures she has filled with the flesh of men as stones!
O fatal eagerness!

2

O boy, their childhood was like so many oatmeal cookies.
I need you, you need me, yum, yum. Anon it became suddenly

3

like someone always losing something and never knowing what.
Always so. They were so fond of eating bread and butter and
sugar, they were slobs, the mice used to lick the floorboards
after they went to bed, rolling their light tails against
the rattling marbles of granulation. Vivo! the dextrose
those children consumed, lavished, smoked, in their knobby
candy bars. Such pimples! such hardons! such moody loves.
And thus they grew like giggling fir trees.

*Easter*

The razzle dazzle maggots are summary
tattooing my simplicity on the pitiable.
The perforated mountains of my saliva leave cities awash
more exclusively open and more pale than skirts.
O the glassy towns are fucked by yaks
slowly bleeding a quiet filigree on the leaves of that souvenir
of a bird chastely crossing the boulevard of falling stars
cold in the dull heavens
drowned in flesh,
it's the night like I love it all cruisy and nelly
fingered fan of boskage fronds the white smile of sleeps.

When the world strips down and rouges up
like a mattress's teeth brushed by love's bristling sun
a marvellous heart tiresomely got up in brisk bold stares
when those trappings fart at the feet of the stars
a self-coral serpent wrapped round an arm with no jujubes
without swish
without camp
floods of crocodile piss and pleasures of driving
shadows of prairie pricks dancing
of the roses of Pennsylvania looking in eyes noses and ears
those windows at the head of science.
I supplicate
dirty blonde mermaids leaning on their elbows
rigor mortis sculpting the figure of those iron tears,
all the feathers falling font a sea of yuccas and blue riddles
every Nevada fantastic has lost his dolorous teeth
when the world, smutty abstract, powders its pearls
the gardens of the sea's come
a mast of the barcantine lost flaming bearer of hurricanes
a hardon a sequoia a toilet tissue
a reject of poor people
in squeezing your deflowered eyeballs
all the powdered and pomaded balloon passengers
voluntarily burning their orifices to a cinder
a short circuit in the cow eyes' sour milk
eyes sucked by fever
the x-ray night's mercury prophylaxis
women who use cigars
the sea swallowing tumultuous islands
is burnt by the sun like a girl
a sieve of stinking villages
a muff of mosquitoes in the walking dark
pouring demented chinchillas
trumpets fell, many the virulent drapery lids
the murdered raining softly on yellow oranges
violating the opaque sexual privileges of twilight
the big nigger of noon
just as the floor of the ocean crushes pebbles

too eager for the appetites of little feet.
Giving and getting the pubic foliage of precarious hazard
sailors
Silent ripples in a bayou of raffish bumpkin winks
sweet meat packers touting the herb bracelets of pus
kisses! kisses!
fresher than the river that runs like a moon through girls.
And the swamped ship flouncing to the portholes at the eagle hour
earrings

the ship sawed up by the biting asses of stars
at the heaving buttocks of coupling drydocks
and the ship latches onto a sideboard of sourdough
sends telegrams by camel and dodo
an aloof dancer practicing push-ups on top of the mast
all night you see them plunging and swizzling
pouncing elegantly in that jewelled grass
an army of frigates
an army of cocks
an army of wounds
an army of young married couples' vanilla hemorrhages
a spine-tingling detonation nested in leaves
alfalfa blowing against sisters in a hanky of shade
and the tea-ship crushes an army of hair
in rampant jaws those streets whose officer deploys a day of
hairs strutting the rosy municipal ruts
hairs brushing the seaflowers and tapestries from the gums
of the shore

birdie, birdie
on the uptown train
dining in the midst of waiters
O the bread of colleens butters the rain.
A minute more and earth would grab the crater's lip
and a wind of diamonds rough up red sultans
and their cast off whores, chemises!
shuffling their shoes to a milky number about sugar
in the gardens of the rainbow planted by anarchists

whose hairy sheets cover the nits of canaries
brushed out by henna specialists.
When the world has walked the tightrope that ties up our eyes
when the world has stretched the rubber skin of sleep
when the world is just a cluttered box for your cluttered box
and charges through the cream of your smiling entrails
like a Pope
sounding box of tomorrow champion box alarm
at the call of mystics and pilots
box raining sadly over Sicily and over the bars
and the weekly tooth brush

furious senses your lianas forest the virgin
O sins of sex and kisses of birds at the end of the penis
cry of a black princess whose mouth founders in the Sun
a million gardens fill the white furry sky
black pillow cast on the retreating flood of night
absurd ice under the hand's breast of dark
bitten by smiles habitual, the giggle
in the blue lidded eyes of prunes
a dawn of justice and magnetic mines
the princess in the clear heart of summer sucks her flower
and honey drowns her in a green valley
she is privately caught in the breeze blown silence
night without eyelids
tied to the jet of my mysterious galley
my cuckoo my boomerang
I have sunk my tongue in the desperation of her blood
strangely her features are Easter
and the balm of Easter floods, my tongue's host
a rivulet of purple blood runs over the wise hands
of sobbing infants.
And the ship shoves off into the heady oceans of love
whose limpidity is the exile of the self
I cry the moon to shower fishes and tears over her
runners through the warring surf of Red Indians
on the California shore, that nausea
not swamp the wind's hands of the Sun

towering afire over the living islands and hairy waves
not forgotten in the silken sound of fruits
proud shout the coyotes and the orchids of the testicles.

Boom of pregnant hillsides
awash with urine
a tambourine relieving the earth beside a hedge
when the fingers tap against the spine it's cherry time
where are the suburbs of powdered corpses dancing
O the amusing audience to all words shivers
before the flashing sword of the thighs of the Sun
like a hangar the sun fries all mumbojumboes
and the rivers scramble like lizards about the ankle
until the ravishing pronunciamento of stone.

Black bastard black prick black pirate whose cheek
batters the heavenly heart
and signs its purple in the ribs of nightly explosion
Sun boom
sleep trooped about by paid assassins mad for kisses
from the bamboo bottle of the Father of Heaven, race
whom I quit as the salamander quits the flame.
The day passes into the powdery light of your embrace
like an Alaskan desert over the basket of Mexico
before the coming of the Spics. River rushing into the Sun
to become golden and drossy drip the fingernails
the molluscs on the underside of the scrotum
embroidered with lice and saliva and berries
the Sun sings in the stones of the savage
when the world booms its seven cunts
like a river plunged upon and perishing
Sun, to the feast!
to be pelted by the shit of the stars at last in flood
like a breath.

# ROBERT DUNCAN

born 1919

## *Eyesight II*

The eye opening is a mouth seeing,
an organ of sight gasping for air.
Love in the eye corrupts the seed
stirring new freaks of vision there.

How wonderful in the new sight the world will appear!

The mouth speaking is a heart breathing
The blood itself has seen something.
The world worm changing, coiled in his pit,
is the ripeness of the fruit, the organ of sight.

How wonderful in the new eye the world will appear!


## *Turning into*

turning into a restful roomfull;
turning into a guide to the book;
turning into a man-naked memory;
turning into a long avenue;
turning into a lady reclining;
turning into a mother declining;
turning into a vegetable declaiming;
turning into a yesterday for tomorrow;
turning into an age old sorrow;
turning into a cat fit for fiddling;
turning into a wheel withering;
turning into a god whose heart's at ease;
turning into an hour of sore dis-ease;
turning into an eagle bottle January;

turning into a hairy baby song;
turning into an all nite long;
turning into a doctor's office;
turning into a rubber grimace;
turning into a snail's pace,
        a rail's distance, a long face;
turning into a turn with grace.


## Coming out of

coming out of the house to die;
coming out a babe's first cry;
coming out of a swollen eye;
coming out of the belief in Jehovah;
coming out of the store on the corner;
coming out of his acquaintance with a convict;
coming out of a serious conviction;
coming out of a lover's communion;
coming out of so very little;
coming out of neighbor's tittle tattle;
coming out of a hole in a rattle;
coming out of stupid associations;
coming out of exhausted vacations;
coming out of six-foot relations;
coming out of church on Sunday;
coming out of Wednesday and Monday;
coming out of exorbitant reading;
coming out of a swoon from bleeding;
coming out of a fanciful rain;
coming out of a doll in vain;
coming out again and again.

# KENNETH KOCH

born 1924

## You Were Wearing

You were wearing your Edgar Allan Poe printed cotton blouse.

In each divided up square of the blouse was a picture of Edgar Allan Poe.

Your hair was blonde and you were cute. You asked me, 'Do most boys think that most girls are bad?'

I smelled the mould of your seaside resort hotel bedroom on your hair held in place by a John Greenleaf Whittier clip.

'No,' I said, 'it's girls who think that boys are bad.' Then we read *Snowbound* together

And ran around in an attic, so that a little of the blue enamel was scraped off my George Washington, Father of His Country, shoes.


Mother was walking in the living room, her Strauss Waltzes comb in her hair.

We waited for a time and then joined her, only to be served tea in cups painted with pictures of Herman Melville

As well as with illustrations from his book *Moby Dick* and from his novella, *Benito Cereno*.

Father came in wearing his Dick Tracy necktie: 'How about a drink, everyone?'

I said, 'Let's go outside a while.' Then we went onto the porch and sat on the Abraham Lincoln swing.

You sat on the eyes, mouth, and beard part, and I sat on the knees.

In the yard across the street we saw a snowman holding a garbage can lid smashed into a likeness of the mad English king, George the Third.

# JOHN ASHBERY

born 1927

*Le Livre est sur la table*

## I

All beauty, resonance, integrity,
Exist by deprivation or logic
Of strange position. This being so,

We can only imagine a world in which a woman
Walks and wears her hair and knows
All that she does not know. Yet we know

What her breasts are. And we give fullness
To the dream. The table supports the book,
The plume leaps in the hand. But what

Dismal scene is this? the old man pouting
At a black cloud, the woman gone
Into the house, from which the wailing starts?

## II

The young man places a bird-house
Against the blue sea. He walks away
And it remains. Now other

Men appear, but they live in boxes.
The sea protects them like a wall.
The gods worship a line-drawing

Of a woman, in the shadow of the sea
Which goes on writing. Are there
Collisions, communications on the shore

Or did all secrets vanish when
The woman left? Is the bird mentioned
In the waves' minutes, or did the land advance?


## Grand Abacus

Perhaps this valley too leads into the head of long-ago days.

What, if not its commercial and etiolated visage, could break through the meadow wires?

It placed a chair in the meadow and then went far away.

People come to visit in summer, they do not think about the head.

Soldiers come down to see the head. The stick hides from them.

The heavens say, 'Here I am, boys and girls!'

The stick tries to hide in the noise. The leaves, happy, drift over the dusty meadow.

'I'd like to see it,' someone said about the head, which has stopped pretending to be a town.

Look! A ghastly change has come over it. The ears fall off – they are laughing people.

The skin is perhaps children, they say, 'We children,' and are vague near the sea. The eyes –

Wait! What large raindrops! The eyes –

Wait, can't you see them pattering, in the meadow, like a dog?

The eyes are all glorious! And now the river comes to sweep away the last of us.

Who knew it, at the beginning of the day?

It is best to travel like a comet, with the others, though one does not see them.

How far that bridle flashed! 'Hurry up, children!' The birds fly back, they say, 'We were lying,

We do not want to fly away.' But it is already too late. The children have vanished.

### 'They dream only of America'

They dream only of America
To be lost among the thirteen million pillars of grass:
'This honey is delicious
*Though it burns the throat.*'

And hiding from darkness in barns
They can be grownups now
And the murderer's ash tray is more easily –
The lake a lilac cube.

He holds a key in his right hand.
'Please,' he asked willingly.
He is thirty years old.
That was before

We could drive hundreds of miles
At night through dandelions.
When his headache grew worse we
Stopped at a wire filling station.

Now he cared only about signs.
Was the cigar a sign?
And what about the key?
He went slowly into the bedroom.

'I would not have broken my leg if I had not fallen
Against the living room table. What is it to be back
Beside the bed? There is nothing to do
For our liberation, except wait in the horror of it.

And I am lost without you.'

## Poem

While we were walking under the top
The road so strangely lit by lamps
And I wanting only peace
From the tradesmen who tried cutting my hair
Under their lips a white word is waiting
Hanging from a cliff like the sky

It is because of the sky
We ever reached the top
On that day of waiting
For the hand and the lamps
I moisten my crystal hair
Never so calmly as when at peace

With the broken sky of peace
Peace means it to the sky
Let down your hair
Through peaceful air the top
Of ruins because what are lamps
When night is waiting

A room of people waiting
To die in peace
Then strike the procession of lamps
They brought more than sky
Lungs back to the top
Means to doom your hair

Those bright pads of hair
Before the sea held back waiting
And you cannot speak to the top
It moves toward peace
And know the day of sky
Only by falling lamps

Beyond the desert lamps
Mount enslaved crystal mountains of hair
Into the day of sky
Silence is waiting
For anything peace
And you find the top

The top is lamps
Peace to the fragrant hair
Waiting for a tropical sky

# H. R. HAYS

born 1904

## *January*

The air is
Sucked clear of dross.
Space is enlarged.
A hundred miles away
Birds are whistling
And I know
That time is pale blue.

If I throw a stone
It will disappear,
Snatched by a yellow hand
With burnished nails.

Sunlight and stillness,
Creeping along the branches,
Nest in the pine needles.

Ponds stare at the sky
Through opaque, glittering spectacles
And do not reflect
The skeletons of angels,
Picnicing in
Refracted light.

The cold has
Bathed my eyeballs with tears
As I stare into the crevices
Of an ancient Paradise.

Breathe in,
Breathe out.

## The Sacred Children

Children believe in clover, magic numbers,
And wish on falling stars.
They are afraid of cracks in sidewalks,
Dangerous Fridays, they worship
Luck in mirrors, months,
And the coming of white horses.

Shadows are large in the minds of children,
Moving in mystic and primal algebras
That shall solve sunrise. Signs make a music
Of warning and praise.

Oh there are marvels in the souls of children –
Prophetic insects, stones that grow. They see
Life in a drowned hair
And know that death flies into rooms
On a bird's wings.

## The Case

The night Las Vegas caught fire
The air was full of money.

Operative X5 discovered
Traces of strontium in the urine
Of the secretary of state.

The sea was cold that year,
Dark, spiny shapes were seen
Waving their tentacles.
Flung on shore, they melted
Leaving a yellow stain.

A device was perfected
To control the sex of unborn infants
And to endow them all with photoelectric cells.

Operative X5 was decapitated,
Brainwashed, shot through the heart,
His balls cut off.
After a cold shower, he gunned his motor
And drove westward
At eighty miles an hour.

An enormous eye,
Glossy as a fried egg,
Appeared at the zenith
And stared at the earth
For hours on end.
Sometimes sunset lasted until morning.

Operative X5 entered his
Space capsule, a girl
With red hair came to meet him.
He knew all about her.
With one hand he unzipped his fly,
With the other he
Cut her throat.

Yet all over the country
Grass still grew on the telephone wires
And moths with a six-foot wingspread
Soared over Lake Erie
And settled on Buffalo.

Operative X5 stripped the plastic
Mask from his face revealing the wires,
The rusting mechanism
And the body of a dead rat.

Once more horse-drawn trolleys
Appeared in the streets.
Frontal lobotomy was performed
On every male American
With an I.Q. of over a hundred —
The case was solved.

But no one could understand why the brittle
Skeletons of birds
Fell like snowflakes.
Fell continually.


## Manhattan

I have eaten the city.
I see myself in a thousand doorways,
Simply as light,
Single as crowds;
The air extinguishes my footsteps.
My skin surrounds the shadow of the monument.

The long afternoon,
Burning with women's beautiful dresses,
Flows with the tides of my blood.
Among the public privacies of the sunset,
I can hear dust falling.
The shadow of voices
Struggles to rise
Like a bird without wings.

I have eaten the city.
Surrounded by musical silence,
I have swallowed crowds of pigeons,
Grass grows on my eyelids,
My body is full of windows.

## For One Who Died Young

He went into a grey day,
A damp wind filling the sails
With mirrors;
He went into the strange
Salt film of memory
Where he makes familiar gestures
Eternally.

He left us the print
Of his bare foot in the sand;
He left us summer and sorrow,
He left us a hammer and saw,
He left us twelve o'clock,
Rhododendrons, high tides and leaves
That fall in autumn.
He left us empty shells
Echoing with the sound of the heart.

He leaned against the clouds
In which the shape
Of his shadow remains.
His laughter told the time of day,
His silences
Were brown with the color of earth.
He gathered minutes with both hands
And paid with the coin
Of his blood.

When we drink glasses of water,
When we wind our watches,
When we open and close doors,
When we light fires and post letters,
We speak to him and he answers.

# ROBERT BLY

born 1926

## *Waking from Sleep*

Inside the veins there are navies setting forth,
Tiny explosions at the water lines,
And seagulls weaving in the wind of the salty blast.

It is the morning. The country has slept the whole winter.
Window seats were covered with fur skins, the yard was full
Of stiff dogs, and hands that clumsily held heavy books.

Now we wake, and rise from bed, and eat breakfast —
Shouts rise from the harbour of the blood,
Mist, and masts rising, the knock of wooden tackle in the sunlight.

Now we sing, and do tiny dances on the kitchen floor.
Our whole body is like a harbour at dawn;
We know that our master has left us for the day.

## *Snowfall in the Afternoon*

### I

The grass is half-covered with snow.
It was the sort of snowfall that starts in late afternoon,
And now the little houses of the grass are growing dark.

### II

If I reached my hands down, near the earth,
I could take handfuls of darkness!
A darkness was always there, which we never noticed.

### III

As the snow grows heavier, the cornstalks fade farther away,
And the barn moves nearer to the house.
The barn moves all alone in the growing storm.

### IV

The barn is full of corn, and moving towards us now,
Like a hulk blown towards us in a storm at sea;
All the sailors on deck have been blind for many years.

## *At a March against the Vietnam War*

Washington, 27 November 1965

Newspapers rise high in the air over Maryland

We walk about, bundled in coats
    and sweaters in the late November sun

Looking down, I see feet moving
Calmly, gaily,
Almost as if separated from their bodies

But there is something moving in the dark somewhere
Just beyond
The edge of our eyes: a boat
Covered with machine guns
Moving along under trees

It is black,
The hand reaches out
And cannot touch it –
It is that darkness among pine boughs
That the Puritans brushed
As they went out to kill turkeys

At the edge of the jungle clearing
It explodes
On the ground

We long to abase ourselves

We have carried around this cup of darkness
We have longed to pour it over our heads

We make war
Like a man anointing himself

## Counting Small-Boned Bodies

Let's count the bodies over again.

If we could only make the bodies smaller,
The size of skulls,
We could make a whole plain white with skulls in the moonlight!

If we could only make the bodies smaller,
Maybe we could get
A whole year's kill in front of us on a desk!

If we could only make the bodies smaller,
We could fit
A body into a finger-ring, for a keepsake forever.

# [PABLO NERUDA]

## 1904–1973

### *Walking Around*

It so happens I am sick of being a man.
And it happens that I walk into tailorshops and movie houses
dried up, waterproof, like a swan made of felt
steering my way in a water of wombs and ashes.

The smell of barbershops makes me break into hoarse sobs.
The only thing I want is to lie still like stones or wool.
The only thing I want is to see no more stores, no gardens,
no more goods, no spectacles, no elevators.

It so happens I am sick of my feet and my nails
and my hair and my shadow.
It so happens I am sick of being a man.

Still it would be marvelous
to terrify a law clerk with a cut lily,
or kill a nun with a blow on the ear.
It would be great
to go through the streets with a green knife
letting out yells until I died of the cold.

I don't want to go on being a root in the dark,
insecure, stretched out, shivering with sleep,
going on down, into the moist guts of the earth,
taking in and thinking, eating every day.

I don't want so much misery.
I don't want to go on as a root and a tomb,
alone under the ground, a warehouse with corpses,
half frozen, dying of grief.

That's why Monday, when it sees me coming
with my convict face, blazes up like gasoline,
and it howls on its way like a wounded wheel,
and leaves tracks full of warm blood leading toward the night.

And it pushes me into certain corners, into some moist houses,
into hospitals where the bones fly out the window,
into shoeshops that smell like vinegar,
and certain streets hideous as cracks in the skin.

There are sulphur-colored birds, and hideous intestines
hanging over the doors of houses that I hate,
and there are false teeth forgotten in a coffeepot,
there are mirrors
that ought to have wept from shame and terror,
there are umbrellas everywhere, and venoms, and umbilical cords.

I stroll along serenely, with my eyes, my shoes,
my rage, forgetting everything,
I walk by, going through office buildings and orthopedic shops,
and courtyards with washing hanging from the line:
underwear, towels and shirts from which slow
dirty tears are falling.

(*Translated from the Spanish by Robert Bly*)

[PABLO NERUDA]

*Nothing but Death*

There are cemeteries that are lonely,
graves full of bones that do not make a sound,
the heart moving through a tunnel,
in it darkness, darkness, darkness,
like a shipwreck we die going into ourselves,
as though we were drowning inside our hearts,
as though we lived falling out of the skin into the soul.

And there are corpses,
feet made of cold and sticky clay,
death is inside the bones,
like a barking where there are no dogs,
coming out from bells somewhere, from graves somewhere,
growing in the damp air like tears or rain.

Sometimes I see alone
coffins under sail,
embarking with the pale dead, with women that have dead hair,
with bakers who are as white as angels,
and pensive young girls married to notary publics,
caskets sailing up the vertical river of the dead,
the river of dark purple,
moving upstream with sails filled out by the sound of death,
filled by the sound of death which is silence.

Death arrives among all that sound
like a shoe with no foot in it, like a suit with no man in it,
comes and knocks, using a ring with no stone in it, with no finger
    in it,
comes and shouts with no mouth, with no tongue, with no throat.
Nevertheless its steps can be heard
and its clothing makes a hushed sound, like a tree.

I'm not sure, I understand only a little, I can hardly see,
but it seems to me that its singing has the color of damp violets,
of violets that are at home in the earth,
because the face of death is green,
and the look death gives is green,
with the penetrating dampness of a violet leaf
and the somber color of embittered winter.

But death also goes through the world dressed as a broom,
lapping the floor, looking for dead bodies,
death is inside the broom,
the broom is the tongue of death looking for corpses,
it is the needle of death looking for thread.

Death is inside the folding cots:
it spends its life sleeping on the slow mattresses,
in the black blankets, and suddenly breathes out:
it blows out a mournful sound that swells the sheets,
and the beds go sailing toward a port
where death is waiting, dressed like an admiral.

(Translated from the Spanish by Robert Bly)

## [PABLO NERUDA]

### Ode to the Watermelon

The tree of intense
summer,
hard,
is all blue sky,
yellow sun,
fatigue in drops,
a sword
above the highways,
a scorched shoe
in the cities:
the brightness and the world
weigh us down,
hit us
in the eyes
with clouds of dust,
with sudden golden blows,
they torture
our feet
with tiny thorns,
with hot stones,
and the mouth
suffers

more than all the toes:
the throat
becomes thirsty,
the teeth,
the lips, the tongue:
we want to drink
waterfalls,
the dark blue night,
the South Pole,
and then
the coolest of all
the planets crosses
the sky,
the round, magnificent,
star-filled watermelon.

It's a fruit from the thirst-tree.
It's the green whale of the summer.

The dry universe
all at once
given dark stars
by this firmament of coolness
lets the swelling
fruit
come down:
its hemispheres open
showing a flag
green, white, red,
that dissolves into
wild rivers, sugar,
delight!

Jewel box of water, phlegmatic
queen
of the fruitshops,
warehouse
of profundity, moon
on earth!

You are pure,
rubies fall apart
in your abundance,
and we
want
to bite into you,
to bury our
face
in you, and
our hair, and
the soul!
When we're thirsty
we glimpse you
like
a mine or a mountain
of fantastic food,
but
among our longings and our teeth
you change
simply
into cool light
that slips in turn into
spring water
that touched us once
singing.
And that is why
you don't weigh us down
in the siesta hour
that's like an oven,
you don't weigh us down,
you just
go by
and your heart, some cold ember,
turned itself into a single
drop of water.

(*Translated from the Spanish by Robert Bly*)

# [CÉSAR VALLEJO]

1892–1938

## *Poem to be Read and Sung*

I know there is someone
looking for me day and night inside her hand,
and coming upon me, each moment, in her shoes.
Doesn't she know the night is buried
with spurs behind the kitchen?

I know there is someone composed of my pieces,
whom I complete when my waist
goes galloping on her precise little stone.
Doesn't she know that money once out for her likeness
never returns to her trunk?

I know the day,
but the sun has escaped from me;
I know the universal act she performed in her bed
with some other woman's bravery and warm water, whose
shallow recurrence is a mine.
Is it possible this being is so small
even her own feet walk on her that way?

A cat is the border between us two,
right there beside her bowl of water.
I see her on the corners, her dress – once
an inquiring palm tree – opens and closes. . . .
What can she do but change her style of weeping?

But she does look and look for me. This is a real story!

*(Translated from the Spanish by James Wright and Robert Bly)*

# [CÉSAR VALLEJO]

### '*I have a terrible fear of being an animal*'

I have a terrible fear of being an animal
of white snow, who has kept his father and mother
alive with his solitary circulation through the veins,
and a fear that on this day which is so marvelous, sunny, arch-
    bishoprical,
(a day that stands so for night)
this animal, like a straight line,
will manage not to be happy, or to breathe,
or to turn into something else, or to get money.

It would be a terrible thing
if I were a lot of man up to that point.
Unthinkable nonsense ... an overfertile assumption
to whose accidental yoke the spiritual
hinge in my waist succumbs.
Unthinkable. ... Meanwhile
that's how it is on this side of God's head,
in the tabula of Locke, and of Bacon, in the pale neck
of the beast, in the snout of the soul.

And, in fragrant logic,
I do have that practical fear, this marvelous
moony day, of being that one, this one maybe,
to whose nose the ground smells like a corpse,
the unthinkable alive and the unthinkable dead.

Oh to roll on the ground, to be there, to cough, to wrap oneself,
to wrap the doctrine, the temple, from shoulder to shoulder,
to go away, to cry, to let it go for eight
or for seven or for six, for five, or let it go
for life with its three possibilities!

*(Translated from the Spanish by Robert Bly)*

## [CÉSAR VALLEJO]

### '*And don't bother telling me anything*'

And don't bother telling me anything,
that a man can kill perfectly,
because a man,
sweating ink, does what he can, don't bother telling me . . .

Gentlemen, we'll see ourselves with apples again,
the infant will go by at last,
the expression of Aristotle fortified
with huge wooden hearts,
and Heraclitus's grafted on to Marx's,
the suave one's sounding abrupt . . .
My own throat used to tell me that all the time:
a man can kill perfectly.

Sirs
and gentlemen, we'll see ourselves without packages again:
until that time I ask, from my inadequacy I would like to know
the day's tone, which,
as I see it, has already been here waiting for me in my bed.
And I demand of my hat the doomed analogy of memory,
since at times I assume my wept-for and immense space, success-
    fully,
since at times I drown in the voice of my neighbor,
and I suffer
counting the years like corn grains,
brushing off my clothes to the sound of a corpse,
or sitting drunk in my coffin . . .

(*Translated from the Spanish by Robert Bly*)

## [CÉSAR VALLEJO]

### 'The anger that breaks a man down into boys'

The anger that breaks a man down into boys,
that breaks the boy down into equal birds,
and the bird, then, into tiny eggs;
the anger of the poor
owns one smooth oil against two vinegars.

The anger that breaks the tree down into leaves,
and the leaf down into different-sized buds,
and the buds into infinitely fine grooves;
the anger of the poor
owns two rivers against a number of seas.

The anger that breaks the good down into doubts,
and doubt down into three matching arcs,
and the arc, then, into unimaginable tombs;
the anger of the poor
owns one piece of steel against two daggers.

The anger that breaks the soul down into bodies,
the body down into different organs,
and the organ into reverberating octaves of thought;
the anger of the poor
owns one deep fire against two craters.

(*Translated from the Spanish by Robert Bly*)

## [TOMAS TRANSTRÖMER]

born 1931

### Track

2 AM: moonlight. The train has stopped
out in a field. Far off sparks of light from a town,
flickering coldly on the horizon.

As when a man goes so deep into his dream
he will never remember that he was there
when he returns again to his room.

Or when a person goes so deep into a sickness
that his days all become some flickering sparks, a swarm,
feeble and cold on the horizon.

The train is entirely motionless.
2 o'clock: strong moonlight, few stars.

*(Translated from the Swedish by Robert Bly)*


## [TOMAS TRANSTRÖMER]

### The Man Awakened by a Song Above His Roof

Morning, May rain. The city is silent still
as a sheepherder's hut. Streets silent. And in
the sky a plane motor is rumbling bluish-green. –
The window is open.

The dream of the man stretched out sleeping
becomes at that instant transparent. He turns, begins
to grope for the tool of his consciousness. –
Almost in space.

*(Translated from the Swedish by Robert Bly)*

# [TOMAS TRANSTRÖMER]

### Allegro

After a black day, I play Haydn,
and feel a little warmth in my hands.

The keys are ready. Kind hammers fall.
The sound is spirited, green, and full of silence.

The sound says that freedom exists
and someone pays no tax to Caesar.

I shove my hands in my haydnpockets
and act like a man who is calm about it all.

I raise my haydnflag. The signal is:
'We do not surrender. But want peace.'

The music is a house of glass standing on a slope;
rocks are flying, rocks are rolling.

The rocks roll straight through the house
but every pane of glass is still whole.

(*Translated from the Swedish by Robert Bly*)

# [TOMAS TRANSTRÖMER]

## *Open and Closed Space*

With his work, as with a glove, a man feels the universe.
At noon he rests a while, and lays the gloves aside on a shelf.
There they suddenly start growing, grow huge
and make the whole house dark from inside.

The darkened house is out in the April winds.
'Amnesty,' the grass whispers, 'amnesty.'
A boy runs along with an invisible string which goes right up
    into the sky.
There his wild dream of the future flies like a kite, bigger than his
    town.

Farther to the north, you see from a hill the blue matting of fir
    trees
on which the shadows of the clouds
do not move.
No, they are moving.

*(Translated from the Swedish by Robert Bly)*

## *An Extra Joyful Chorus for Those Who Have Read This Far*

I sit alone late at night.
I sit with eyes closed, thoughts shoot through me.
I am not floating, but fighting.
In the marshes the mysterious mother calls to her moor-bound
    chicks.
I love the Mother.
I am an enemy of the Mother, give me my sword.
I leap into her mouth full of seaweed.

I am the single splinter that shoots through the stratosphere leaving
    fire trails!
I walk upright, robes flapping at my heels,
I am fleeing along the ground like a frightened beast.
I am the ball of fire the woodman cuts out of the wolf's stomach,
I am the sun that floats over the Witch's house,
I am the horse sitting in the chestnut tree singing,
I am the man locked inside the oakwomb,
waiting for lightning, only let out on stormy nights.
I am the steelhead trout that hurries to his mountain mother,
to live again in the stream where he was born,
gobbling up the new water.


Sometimes when I read my own poems late at night,
I sense myself on a long road,
I feel the naked thing alone in the universe,
the hairy body padding in the fields at dusk . . .


I have floated in the eternity of the cod heaven,
I have felt the silver of infinite numbers brush my side –
I am the crocodile unrolling and slashing through the mudded
    water
I am the baboon crying out as her baby falls from the tree,
I am the light that makes the flax blossom at midnight!
I am an angel breaking into three parts over the Ural Mountains!
I am no one at all.

*

I am a thorn enduring in the dark sky,
I am the one whom I have never met,
I am a swift fish shooting through the troubled waters,
I am the last inheritor crying out in deserted houses
I am the salmon hidden in the pool on the temple floor
I am what remains of the beloved
I am an insect with black enamel knees hugging the curve of
    insanity
I am the evening light rising from the ocean plains
I am an eternal happiness fighting in the long reeds.

Our faces shine with the darkness reflected from the Tigris,
cells made by the honeybees that go on growing after death,
a room darkened with curtains made of human hair.

The panther rejoices in the gathering dark.
Hands rush towards each other through miles of space.
All the sleepers in the world join hands.

# GEORGE HITCHCOCK

born 1914

## *The One Whose Reproach I Cannot Evade*

She sits in her glass garden
and awaits the guests –
The sailor with the blue tangerines,
the fish clothed in languages,
the dolphin with a revolver in its teeth.

Dusk enters from stage left:
its voice falls like dew on the arbor.
Tiny bells
sway in the catalpa tree.

What is it she hopes to catch in her net
of love? Petals? Conch-shells?
The night moth? She does not speak.
Tonight, I tell her, no one comes;
you wait in vain.
                Yet at eight precisely
the moon opens its theatric doors,
an arm rises from the fountain,
the music box, face down
on her tabouret, swells and bursts
its cover – a tinkling flood of
rice moves over the table.

She smiles at me, false believer,
smiles and goes in, leaving
the garden empty and my thighs
half-eaten by the raging twilight.

## *The United States Prepare for the Permanent Revolution*

The green shingles of rest homes unfold revealing
    innumerable blonde attics each with a pair
    of pining eyes and an old phonograph
    playing Nights in a Spanish Garden;
Women's handbags open their beaded mouths and utter
    bulletins of rouge and used cleaning tissue;
Various ambiguities take flight from the telephone wires
    and are descried flying southward
    over Cairo, Illinois;
Gospel singers assemble beneath the veiled balconies
    which jut from decayed sopranos;
Dark mornings fall over Seattle.


Terrorists are seen skulking in the public latrines,
    their feet wrapped in soggy vermicelli;
Parking meters rise to heaven chanting the praises
    of unnatural leisure;
tied to a rope of frozen milk a blind man leaps
    from the parapet of Equitable Trust and
    parachutes to safety his descendants hidden
    in the crannies of his venerable beard;
Mauve fungoids scraped from the undersides of pool tables are
    traded for Green Stamps in the Farmers' Market;
Viscosity is proclaimed the prime law of the Universe.


Lighted cigars fall like meteors on a deserted football field
    in Pierre, South Dakota – their entrails are
    officially examined for signs of cancer;
Canvas doorways open in the sails of fishing smacks
    and emit a sour wind;
Groves of carefully marcelled kelp sprout from the armpits
    of the Statue of Liberty;
Flaming poems are inscribed on the groins of mysterious
    black women in straw capes whose thighs
    smell of creosote;

A puma is discovered cowering on the shelves of
    a suburban lending library – in the floodlights
    his tears turn to opals.

A railway flare burns in the bowels of a cuttlefish
    trapped at Sarasota, Florida;
Cases of pomade opened at Nogales for inspection
    are found to contain smoked ice;
A pair of Anglo-Saxon hips is placed on display at
    the Museum of Modern Art.

Dry boards lie at the edge of the road:
Centipedes enter their knotty throats.

What is the recommendation?
Deliberate excision of proud flesh.

    A woman stops me in the corridor.
    Her tongue has been replaced by
    a single mute camellia.


## Song of Expectancy

I wait for her who restores my fingertips
I wait for the moons which will grow on my nails
I wait for the night with its intricate gloves
I wait for the skeleton keys

I wait for the emigrants in glass boats
For the rivers with their green hair
The synagogues which lie just under water
And the jewelled eyes in the willowtree

I wait for the ravens to settle on fencerails
With wings like Finnish wimples
I wait for the pinetrees to explode the stars
And for the clouds with their windows of rain

I wait for the sheriffs who always arrive
With tomorrow manacled between them
I wait for the bandits and their crucified children
Who wear roses of gauze on their masks

For the ragmen who gather our hearts on spikes
The centurions pissing in cemeteries
The cowboys driving cadavers before them
And their yelping mutts whose fur is afire

I wait at last for ignorance and its subpoena
For silence with its headless drum and pews full of empty hats
For sleep which pours in foam from the ribs
And for the dark sad waters where legends swim backward like
    squid

# DONALD HALL

born 1928

## *Je suis une table*

It has happened suddenly,
by surprise, in an arbor,
or while drinking good coffee,
after speaking, or before,

that I dumbly inhabit
a density; in language,
there is nothing to stop it,
for nothing retains an edge.

Simple ignorance presents,
later, words for a function,
but it is common pretense
of speech, by a convention,

and there is nothing at all
but inner silence, nothing
to relieve on principle
now this intense thickening.

## *A Poet at Twenty*

Images leap with him from branch to branch. His eyes
brighten, his head cocks, he pauses under a green bough,
alert.

And when I see him I want to hide him somewhere.

The other wood is past the hill. But he will enter it, and
find the particular maple. He will walk through the door
of the maple, and his arms will pull out of their sockets,
and the blood will bubble from his mouth, his ears, his

penis, and his nostrils. His body will rot. His body will
dry in ropey tatters. Maybe he will grow his body again,
three years later. Maybe he won't.

There is nothing to do, to keep this from happening.

It occurs to me that the greatest gentleness would put
a bullet into his bright eye. And when I look in his eye, it
is not his eye that I see.


## The Alligator Bride

The clock of my days winds down.
The cat eats sparrows outside my window.
Once, she brought me a small rabbit
which we devoured together, under
the Empire Table
while the men shrieked
repossessing the gold umbrella.

Now the beard on my clock turns white.
My cat stares into dark corners
missing her gold umbrella.
She is in love
with the Alligator Bride.

Ah, the tiny fine white
teeth! The Bride, propped on her tail
in white lace
stares from the holes
of her eyes. Her stuck-open mouth
laughs at minister and people.

On bare new wood
fourteen tomatoes,
a dozen ears of corn,
six bottles of white wine,

a melon,
a cat,
broccoli
and the Alligator Bride.

The color of bubble gum,
the consistency of petroleum jelly,
wickedness oozes
from the palm of my left hand.
My cat licks it.
I watch the Alligator Bride.

Big houses like shabby boulders
hold themselves tight
in gelatin.
I am unable to daydream.
The sky is a gun aimed at me.
I pull the trigger.
The skull of my promises
leans in a black closet, gapes
with its good mouth
for a teat to suck.

A bird flies back and forth
in my house that is covered by gelatin
and the cat leaps at it
missing. Under the Empire Table
the Alligator Bride
lies in her bridal shroud.
My left hand
leaks on the Chinese carpet.

## Sudden Things

A storm was coming, that was why it was dark. The wind was blowing the fronds of the palm trees off. They were maples. I looked out the window across the big lawn. The house was huge, full of children and old people. The lion was loose. Either because of the wind, or by male-volent human energy, which is the same thing, the cage had come open. Suppose a child walked outside!

A child walked outside. I knew that I must protect him from the lion. I threw myself on top of the child. The lion roared over me. In the branches and the bushes there was suddenly a loud crackling. The lion cringed. I looked up and saw that the elephant was loose!

The elephant was taller than the redwoods. He was hairy like a mammoth. His tusks trailed vines. Parrots screeched around his head. His eyes rolled crazily. He trumpeted. The ice-cap was breaking up!

The lion backed off, whining. The boy ran for the house. I covered his retreat, locked all the doors and pulled the bars across them. An old lady tried to open a door to get a better look. I spoke sharply to her, she sat down grumbling and pulled a blanket over her knees.

Out of the window I saw zebras and rattlesnakes and wildebeests and cougars and woodchucks on the lawns and in the tennis courts. I worried how, after the storm, we would put the animals back in their cages, and get to the mainland.

# JOHN PERREAULT

born 1937

## *Boomerang*

Why is everything I do in my life like a boomerang?
I throw the paper airplane out the window
and the wind sends it back.
I spit against the wind.

You bought me a fur boomerang for my birthday.
I hate you now. You are so rich.
You are such a consumer.
And I hate your boomerang.
But I can't throw it away.
It keeps coming back and hitting me
in the back of the head.

In a rooming house I lived in once
I knew a boy who had a handmade boomerang.
It was fifteen inches long.
What a beautiful gigantic handmade boomerang!
Every Sunday he practiced throwing it away,
in Central Park, by that sailboat lake.

People always talked to him and followed him.
Everybody wanted to see his boomerang.

... But boomerangs are dangerous.
When you fool around with boomerangs
you have to know what you're doing.

Congratulations, incidentally, on the birth
of your brand new baby boy boomerang.
How amazing
that no matter where you leave him
in the morning he is always
in that basket, on your doorstep.

I had a dream about a boomerang race.
I lost.

But do I really know what it means?
Do I know what anything means?

I kiss your amorous aluminum boomerang
and the edges are so sharp
my tongue gets sliced,
my words get sliced
and my lips are able to smile in two directions.

And I think it would be nice to own a boomerang store.
Glass boomerangs.
Australian aborigine boomerangs.
Rubber safety boomerangs.
Regulation boomerangs for boomerang contests.
And even
automatic talking doll boomerangs.

But why is everything I do in my life like a boomerang?
I throw away my life
and my life comes back.


### Readymade

#### The Venus Fly Trap

(1) A Beautiful Plant!

Its dark green leaves form a low symmetrical rosette.
Each leaf is tipped with a lovely pink trap.


(2) Eats Flies And Insects!

Each pink trap contains a bit of nectar. It is this color and sweetness which attracts the unsuspecting insect. Once he enters the trap, it snaps shut. Digestive juices then dissolve him.

### (3) Eats Flies And Insects!

When the insect has been completely absorbed, the trap reopens and prettily awaits another morsel.

### (4) A Beautiful Plant!

Traps will bite *at* – but not *off* – 'more than they can chew.'

### (5) Feed It Raw Beef!

If there are no insects in your house, you can feed the traps tiny slivers of raw beef. The plant will thrive on such food.

### (6) Instructive For Children!

Youngsters especially will enjoy growing these exotic plants. And if, somehow, you can convey the thought that many of life's alluring enticements can prove to be traps, you will have made a priceless investment!

### (7) Easy To Grow!

They thrive in glass containers and develop traps in three to four weeks. They will beautify any room in your house.

### *Shoe*

A road can't be as sad as a shoe is sad
when a shoe can't read.
I can't read either.

And I have given away all my clothes
and gone away so far
that no one will even remember that I've gone
nor how far I went when I was here.

For a road can't be as crazy as a ranch is mad
when a ranch can't sing.

I cough. I spit. I jump up and down
and I run around like a headless rooster.

Me too. I am not lonesome. I am gregarious.
I make friends with the curbstone even.

But a shoe can't be as pretty as a wheel when it's turning
or a tunnel uncovered by chance.
And a shoe can't be a lobster.

I am as free as a belt or a bell or
a dog on a leash
gone crazy with the aroma of flagpoles.


## The Metaphysical Paintings

### 1. The Enigma of Arrival

We are nude beneath our costumes
as in the false myths we have been forced
to memorize
and there is a mistake in your eyes.

We are not aware that at last
the last official has arrived.

Since the sky is false
I tell you falsely of my absence of feelings.

And you stand there staring down
counting the toes
that peek from out beneath
the hem of your theatrical robe.


### 2. *The Melancholy of an Afternoon*

The two of us make love
in the form of identical vegetables,
in shade,
oblivious to noise
and vanishing parades,
oblivious to flags
or that which tries to harm us
from the top of the industrial tower.


### 3. *A Grand Tour*

A mistake. It is a tower and not a tour
that does not crumble.
And we will make arrangements now
to take a guided tour of this tower
and soon find out that there are no stairs
and when you get to the top
there is no view.


### 4. *Departure of a Friend*

I see you lying on a candy-striped towel
face-down,
reading a book of small pictures,
a book about Michelangelo.

Goodbye.

But the time is wrong.
We discover that the train has already left.

It is a false goodbye.
Our shadows become one long shadow
that touches a pool.

Why is it that the railroad station is at times
so quiet? So empty?

### 5. *Nostalgia for the Infinite*

I will miss your loose-leaf notebooks
and your figs.
I will miss your calculated mistakes
and the pictures you sometimes liked to take.

We are still saying goodbye.
Same time. Same light. Same railroad
station.

Are you about to enter this different tower?
Are you about to become another?
A railroad engineer or a policeman?
Are you about to vanish?

### 6. *Love Song*

O how I have loved you,
O great and classical world,
the way a child loves his father;
but now the time has come
to escape your betrayal.

Only the geometry of a green sphere.
Only the surgery upon a puff of smoke
can save us from more primitive forms
of this industrial sadness!

### 7. *Mystery and Melancholy of a Street*

At that time of day when guardian angels
have retired for the day,
as a small girl with a hoop,
I am menaced by the shadow of a guardian angel.

My substance is of shadow.

I let this angel follow me into the bowels
of an empty moving van;
I am raped by the sun.

I take off my shoes.

I wipe the sweat from his brow
with the hem of my Communion dress.

### 8. *The Enigma of Fate*

One move of the invisible queen,
one shout from the top of the stack,
one hand for the future,
and the spilling of seed.

One road through the labyrinth,
one turn to the left,
and the spilling of seed.

### 9. *Melancholy of an Autumn Afternoon*

We are still saying goodbye.

### 10. *The Naval Barracks*

At an early age, I was expelled
from the Naval Academy.
How well I remember those long Euclidian walks
into the sunset
at the end of a geometrical day.

Accumulations! Neat debris!
The magic of an ammunition dump!

The false perspective of my souvenirs
returns to haunt me.

Patient arrangements of frustrations.
Private mottos.
Public demonstrations of the insatiable
and the obvious!

### 11. *Purity of a Dream*

The purity of my dream can only be maintained
at the expense of the present.

I make a billboard in celebration
of our new found spring.
All the buildings start walking up the highway
to look at it.
They crowd around.

Now that I have made this billboard,
I can carry your picture around in my brain
in a small green suitcase
as I fall asleep
on that small train puffing into the distance.

### 12. *Masks*

I like this room. I like this movie of myself.
This view of the antiseptic town.

You are my mask
and I am yours.

Empty!

### 13. *Hector and Andromache*

At last we are together. Our dreams like our shadows
have at last combined.
We observe the higher mathematics
of our consistent departure.

We interfuse.

The geometry of our inter-relationship
has become like the demolished city
and the preserved city –

a train station that arrows towards
a new release of political crime,
a vertical of deliverance.

# BILL KNOTT

born 1940

### (*End*) *of Summer* (*1966*)

I'm tired of murdering children.
Once, long ago today, they wanted to live;
now I feel Vietnam the place
where rigor mortis is beginning to set-in upon me.

I force silence down the throats of mutes,
down the throats of mating-cries of animals who know they are
    extinct.
The chameleon's death-soliloquy is your voice's pulse;
your scorched forehead a constellation's suicide-note.

A phonograph needle plunges through long black hair,
and stone drips slowly into our veins.
The earth has been squandered by the meek.
And upsidedown in the earth a dead man walks upon my soles
    when I walk.

A baby is crying.
In the swaddling-pages
a baby.

'Don't cry. No Solomon's-sword can
divide you from the sky.
You are one. Fly.'

I'm tired, so tired.
I have sleep to do.
I have work to dream.

## Death

Going to sleep, I cross my hands on my chest.
They will place my hands like this.
It will look as though I am flying into myself.

## Sleep

We brush the other, invisible moon.
Its caves come out and carry us inside.

## Hair Poem

Hair is heaven's water flowing eerily over us
Often a woman drifts off down her long hair and is lost

## Poem

At your light side trees shy
A kneeling enters them

## Poem

After your death,
Naomi, your hair will escape to become
a round animal, nameless.

## (Poem) (Chicago) (The Were-Age)

*'My age, my beast!'* — OSIP MANDELSTAM

On the lips a taste of tolling we are blind
The light drifts like dust over faces
We wear masks on our genitals
You've heard of lighting cigarettes with banknotes we used to light
    ours with Jews
History is made of bricks you can't go through it
And bricks are made of bones and blood and
Bones and blood are made of little tiny circles that nothing can go
    through
Except a piano with rabies
Blood gushes into, not from, our wounds
Vietnamese Cuban African bloods
Constellations of sperm upon our bodies
Drunk as dogs before our sons
The bearded foetus lines up at the evolution-trough
Swarmy bloods in the rabid piano
The air over Chicago is death's monogram
This is the Were-Age rushing past
Speed: 10,000 men per minute
This is the species bred of death
The manshriek of flesh
The lifeless sparks of flesh

Covering the deep drums of vision
O new era race-wars jugular-lightning
Dark glance bursting from the over-ripe future
Know we are not the smilelines of dreams
Nor the pores of the Invisible
Piano with rabies we are victorious over
The drum and the wind-chime
We bite back a voice that might have emerged
To tame these dead bodies and wet ashes

## Goodbye

If you are still alive when you read this,
close your eyes. I am
under their lids, growing black.

# KEN SMITH

born 1938

## Train

*After Max Ernst's 'Europe after the Rain'*

In the dark
each sits alone
clutching his flag

I have more than my one death
to attend to
there is a sickness about
and the magician has vanished

But I sit with my twenty six years
spread on my palms
and I wait for the silence
when the programme is interrupted
and the speakers have no script.
And I think how to carry my children
into the sewers.

Roll up the cities.
Let the window explode
in a million glass flowers.
In the darkness already
the woman picking milk from the step
the ashes raked last thing at night
are postures, buried
slipping into dust, rock, ooze,
furniture of a planet
wheeling in silence
lonely as a train
waving its little handkerchiefs of steam

## Possessions

They spent my life plotting against me.
With nothing to do but cultivate themselves,
but to be there, aligning their shadows,
they were planning to undo me,
wanting to own me completely.

They have marched through the rooms,
their presences litter the surfaces
close at my elbow calling attention.
When I sleep they begin with their meetings,
when I leave home they hold a convention.
The minutes, the notes, the chairman
calls order, the lamps signal aye. When I die
they'll start in on another,
easy at first, learning his ways.
Now they're gone, taken from me, good luck.
If I kept them I'd never be free. I'd die
and have to begin picking everything up,
all the waste paper, baby teeth, beards,
I'd have to go back for the fingernails.

So I'm shut of them, all the gossip and malice,
the tables, the chairs with their jokes on me.
All the prying, the scandals. The telephone
stored it all up, the books lied to me.

That's why I came here, bringing nothing.
There was nothing to do but leave things.
I saved only a few: smells of tobacco
and blankets, a dream of a waterfall,
a length of ribbon, my name, my number,
the holes in my suitcase.

# TED BERRIGAN

born 1934

## III

Stronger than alcohol, more great than song,
deep in whose reeds great elephants decay;
I, an island, sail, and my shores toss
on a fragrant evening, fraught with sadness
bristling hate.
It's true, I weep too much. Dawns break
slow kisses on the eyelids of the sea,
what other men sometimes have thought they've seen.
And since then I've been bathing in the poem
lifting her shadowy flowers up for me,
and hurled by hurricanes to a birdless place
the waving flags, nor pass by prison ships
O let me burst, and I be lost at sea!
and fall on my knees then, womanly.

## LXX

*after Arthur Rimbaud*

Sweeter than sour apples flesh to boys
The brine of brackish water pierced my hulk
Cleansing me of rot-gut wine and puke
Sweeping away my anchor in its swell
And since then I've been bathing in the poem
Of the star-steeped milky flowing mystic sea
Devouring great sweeps of azure green and

Watching flotsam, dead men, float by me
Where, dyeing all the blue, the maddened flames
And stately rhythms of the sun, stronger
Than alcohol, more great than song,

Fermented the bright red bitterness of love
I've seen skies split with light, and night,
And surfs, currents, waterspouts; I know
What evening means, and doves, and I have seen
What other men sometimes have thought they've seen


### Bean Spasms

*to George Schneeman*

New York's lovely weather

                hurts my forehead

              in praise of thee
                   the? white dead
                   whose eyes know:

        what are they
of the tiny cloud my brain:
The City's tough red buttons:

              O Mars, red, angry planet,
              candy

                  bar, with sky on top,
      'why, it's young Leander hurrying to his death'
    what? what time is it in New York    in these here alps
  City of lovely tender hate
              and beauty making beautiful
                  old rhymes?
I ran away from you
when you needed something strong
     then I leand against the toilet bowl (ack)
  Malcolm X
        I love my brain
  it all mine now is
saved not knowing
    that &
    that (happily)
    being that:

'wee kill our selves to propagate our kinde'
                                        John Donne

yes, that's true

                        the hair on yr nuts & my
                                big blood-filled cock are a
                                        part in that
                        too


                PART 2

                        Mister Robert Dylan doesn't feel well
                          today
                        That's bad
                        This picture doesn't show that
                        It's not bad, too
                        it's very ritzy in fact
                        here I stand I can't stand
                        to be thing
                        I don't use                 atop
                                the empire state
                                        building
                                                & so sauntered out
                                                that door

That reminds me of the time
I wrote that long piece about a gangster name of 'Jr.'
O Harry James! had eyes to wander but lacked tongue to praise
                                so later peed under his art


                        paused only to lay a sneeze
                                        on Jack Dempsey
                                        asleep with his favorite Horse


                That reminds me of I buzz
                                on & off Miró pop
                                        in & out a Castro convertible
                minute by minute                GENEROSITY!


                                267

Yes now that the seasons totter in their walk
  I do a lot of wondering about Life  in praise of ladies
& Time plaza(s), Bryant Park by the Public    dead of
Library, Smith Bros. black boxes, Times    eye of brow
       Square
      Pirogi Houses
        with long skinny rivers thru
        them
     they lead the weary away
      off! hey!
        I'm no sailor
        off a ship
        at sea  I'M HERE
        & 'The living is easy'
It's 'HIGH TIME'
      & I'm in shapes
      of shadow, they
      certainly can warm, can't they?

  Have you ever seen one?      NO!
       of those long skinny Rivers
        So well hung, in New York
        City
    NO!  in fact
       I'm the Wonderer
& as yr train goes by    forgive me, René! 'just
  I woke up in Heaven       oncet'
      He woke, and wondered more; how
      many angels
   on this train huh?  snore
      for there she lay
  on sheets that mock lust  done that 7 times
        been caught
     and brought back
    to a peach nobody.

To Continue:
Ron Padgett & Ted Berrigan
        hates yr brain
                my dears
                    amidst the many other little buzzes
    & like, Today, as Ron Padgett might say
            is
        'A tub of vodka'
                        'in the morning'
        she might reply
and that keeps it up
        past icy poles
            where angels beg fr doom then zip
                ping in-and-out, joining the army
        wondering about Life
        by the Public Library of
                            Life
                            No Greater Thrill!
        (I wonder)


Now that the earth is changing I wonder what time it's getting
    to be
            sitting on this New York Times Square
        that actually very ritzy, Lauren    it's made of yellow
                                    wood or
            I don't know something        maybe
        This man was my        it's been fluffed up
            friend
            He had a sense for the
                vast            doesn't he?


    Awake my Angel! give thyself
            to the lovely hours    Don't cheat
    The victory is not always to the sweet.
            I mean that.

Now this picture is pretty good here
Though it once got demerits from the lunatic Arthur Cravan
He wasn't feeling good that day
Maybe because he had nothing on
                              paint-wise I mean


                    PART 3
                    I wrote that
                        about what is
                    this empty room      without a heart
                        now in three parts
                    a white flower
                        came home wet & drunk    2 Pepsis
                    and smashed my fist thru her window
                                      in the nude
            As the hand zips you see
                    Old Masters, you can see
                well hung in New York      they grow fast here
                    Conflicting, yet purposeful
                        yet with outcry vain!


                    PART 4
                    Praising, that's it!
you string a sonnet around yr fat gut
    and falling on your knees
                    you invent the shoe
                    for a horse. It brings you luck
                while sleeping
                    'You have it seems a workshop nature'
Have you                'Good Lord!'
                            Some folks is wood
seen them?                 Ron Padgett wd say
                            amidst the many other
                            little buzzes
                    past the neon on & off
                        night & day  STEAK SAND-
                                      WICH

Have you ever tried one Anne? SURE!
'I wonder what time "its"?'
as I sit on this new Doctor
NO     I only look at buildings they're in
as you and he, I mean he & you & I buzz past
in yellow ties     I call that gold
THE HOTEL BUCKINGHAM
(facade) is black, and taller than last time
is looming over lunch   naked   high time   poem   & I, equal in
perfection & desire
is looming   two eyes   over coffee-cup (white) nature
and man:     both hell on poetry.
Art is art and life is
'A monograph on Infidelity'
Oh. Forgive me stench of sandwich
O pneumonia in American Poetry
Do we have time?         well look at Burroughs
7 times been caught and brought back to Mars
& eaten.
'Art is art & Life
is home,' Fairfield Porter said that
turning himself in
Tonight arrives again in red
some go on     even in Colorado                    on the run
the forests shake
meaning:
coffee   the cheerfulness of this poor
fellow is terrible, hidden in
the fringes of the eyelids
blue mysteries' (I'M THE SKY)
The sky is bleeding now
onto 57th Street
of the 20th Century &
HORN & HARDART'S
Right Here. That's PART 5

I'm not some sailor off a ship at sea
I'm the wanderer                                  (age 4)

        & now everyone is dead
          sinking bewildered of hand, of foot, of lip
  nude, thinking
laughter burnished brighter than hate

                              goodbye.
            André Breton said that
                        what a shit!
Now he's gone!
            up bubbles all his amorous breath
          & Monograph on Infidelity entitled
                      The Living Dream
I never again played
                I dreamt that December 27th, 1965
          all in the blazon of sweet beauty's breast

      I mean   'a rose'       Do you understand that?
                   Do you?
   The rock&roll songs of this earth
   commingling absolute joy AND
   incontrovertible joy of intelligence

                     certainly can warm
                can't they?    YES!
           and they do.
      Keeping eternal whisperings around
               (Mr Macadams writes in
               the nude: no that's not
(we want to take the underground  me that: then zips in &
   revolution to Harvard!)     out the boring taxis, re-
                      fusing to join the army
       and yet this girl has   asleep 'on the springs'
        so much grace    of red GENEROSITY)
          I wonder!
      Were all their praises simply prophecies
  of this
      the time!    NO GREATER THRILL
                my friends

But I quickly forget them, those other times, for what are they
but parts in the silver lining of the tiny cloud my brain
drifting up into smoke the city's tough blue top:

        I think a picture always
          leads you gently to someone else
Don't you? like when you ask to leave the room
          & go to the moon.

# TED BERRIGAN and RON PADGETT

## *Orange Jews*

In Wee-John-Boo the bellies of bloodhounds
Resembled John Greenleaf Whittier. Meanwhile
Blood ran like muddy inspiration, forever
Pleasing John Greenleaf Whittier. Meanwhile

Blood ran like muddy inspiration; meanwhile
John Greenleaf Whittier was writing, 'Meanwhile.'
In Wee-John-Boo the mean wiles of John Green
Held no phase for John Greenleaf Whittier.

Francis had not wanted to marry Marvin.
But in 'Meanwhile' by John Greenleaf Whittier, he did.
So Marvin instead married John Greenleaf Whittier's
Father, Cotton Grease Whittier. This pleased John Greenleaf
    Whittier.

Bloodhounds ran after John Greenleaf Whittier's muddy bellies
In Wee-John-Boo, in 'Boo-Boo' by John Greenleaf Whittier.

# RON PADGETT

born 1942

## *After the Broken Arm*

From point A a wind is blowing to point B
Which is here, where the pebble is only a mountain.
If truly heaven and earth are out there
Why is that man waving his arms around,
Gesturing to the word 'lightning' written on the clouds
That surround and disguise his feet?

If you say the right word in New York City
Nothing will happen in New York City;
But out in the fabulous dry horror of the West
A beautiful girl named Sibyl will burst
In by the open window breathless
And settle for an imaginary glass of something.
But now her name is no longer Sibyl – it's Herman,
Yearning for point B.

Dispatch this note to our hero at once.

## *Strawberries in Mexico*

At 14th Street and First Avenue
Is a bank and in the bank the sexiest teller of all time
Next to her the greatest thing about today
Is today itself
Through which I go up
To buy books

They float by under a bluer sky
The girls uptown
Quiet, pampered

The sum of all that's terrible in women
And much of the best

And the old men go by holding small packages
In a trance
So rich even they can't believe it

I think it's a red, white and blue letter day for them too
You see, Con Ed's smokestacks are beautiful
The way Queens is
And horses: from a pleasant distance

Or a fleet of turkeys
Stuffed in a spotless window
In two days they'll be sweating in ovens
Thinking, 'How did I ever get in a fix like this?'

Light pouring over buildings far away

Up here when someone says 'Hey!'
In the street you know they aren't going to kill you
They're yelling to a friend of theirs named Hey
John David Hey, perhaps
And even the garbage goes out
In big white billowy plastic bags tied at the top
Even the people go out in them
Some, now, are waiting
At bus stops (for a probably nonexistent bus . . .)
I thought it was garbage!
It's so pretty!

If you're classless or modern
You can have fun by
Walking into a high-class antique store
So the stately old snob at the desk will ask
In eternity
'You're going where?'
You get to answer 'Up.'

I like these old pricks
If you have an extra hair in the breeze
Their eyes pop out
And then recede way back
As if to say, 'That person is on ... dope!'
They're very correct

But they're not in my shoes
In front of a Dubuffet a circus that shines through
A window in a bright all-yellow building
The window is my eye
And Frank O'Hara is the building
I'm thinking about him like mad today
(As anyone familiar with his poetry will tell)
And about the way Madison Avenue really
Does go to Heaven
And then turns around and comes back, disappointed

Because up here you can sneer at a Negro
Or pity the man
And rent a cloud-colored Bentley and
Architecture's so wonderful!
Why don't I notice it more often?
And the young girls and boys but especially the young girls
Are drifting away from school
In blue and white wool
Wrapped in fur
Are they French? They're speaking French!
And they aren't looking for things to throw
Skirts sliding up the legs of girls who can't keep from grinning
Under beautiful soft brown American eyes
At the whole world
Which includes their plain Jane girlfriends

She even smiled at me!
I have about as much chance of fucking her as the girl at the bank
But I stride along, a terrifying god
Raunchy

A little one day old beard
And good grief I really did forget to brush my teeth this morning
They're turning red with embarrassment
Or is that blood
I've been drinking – I ordered a black coffee
Miss

And then a black policeman comes in
Unbuttoning his uniform at the warmish soda fountain
While I pull the fleece over my teeth
And stare innocently at the books I've bought
One a book with a drawing
By Apollinaire called 'Les fraises au Mexique'
'Strawberries in Mexico'
But when I open the book to that page
It's just a very blue sky I'm looking at


*December*

I will sleep
in my little cup

# TOM CLARK

born 1941

## Superballs

You approach me carrying a book
The instructions you read carry me back beyond birth
To childhood and a courtyard bouncing a ball
The town is silent there is only one recreation
It's throwing the ball against the wall and waiting
To see if it returns
One day
The wall reverses
The ball bounces the other way
Across this barrier into the future
Where it begets occupations names
This is known as the human heart a muscle
A woman adopts it it enters her chest
She falls from a train
The woman rebounds 500 miles back to her childhood
The heart falls from her clothing you retrieve it
Turn it over in your hand the trademark
Gives the name of a noted maker of balls

Elastic flexible yes but this is awful
You say
Her body is limp not plastic
Your heart is missing from it
You replace your heart in your breast and go on your way

## Daily News

Dying day pinches the tot
He grabs my pen and beads
And plays into my hands
His father's skull glistens
Across his wife's white arms

The past bursts on a flower
And softly erases its bulb
We hear this going on all around
Night packs the traffic in cotton
And 1st Ave. fruit stands in opal

It is his first day to hurl a toy
But a gray torch rises in the future
Like a pair of scissors
The dark unravels towards
As I return to my newspaper

## *You (I)*

The door behind me was you
and the radiance, there like
an electric train wreck in your eye
after a horrible evening of waiting outside places in the rain
for you to come
only to
find all of them, two I know, the rest scullions, swimming
around you
in that smoky crowded room like a fishbowl
I escaped from, running away from you and my André Breton
dream of cutting your breasts off with a trowel
and what does that matter to them or to you now, but just
wait it's still early
to the children embroidered in the rug, who seem to be
setting up siege
engines under a tree house full of midgets who look like you.
Where are you in this sky of new blue
deltas I see in the drapery, and your new friends wearing
bamboo singlets
what are they doing down there in the moat waving tridents
like stalks of corn?

Me, I'll be happy to see their blood spilled all over the
$$\text{bedspread}$$
pavilions of your hands as an example. If you come home right
$$\text{now I'll scrunch your hat}$$
between my thighs like a valentine before you have time to
$$\text{wipe them.}$$

## You (II)

You are bright, tremendous, wow.
But it is the hour of one from whom the horrible
$$\text{tremendousness}$$
Of youth is about to depart.
The boats are ready. The air is soft and you perhaps nearby
Do pass, saying 'I am for you'.
This is as much as 'everything is great'.
But desperation builds up all the time.
Life is nothing
    more to me
Strapped at the bottom
    of the throat
Than majesty, I think. You are arduous as that
Ashtray. Swallow me! Since
Your hands are full of streets
And I walk out upon the streets
And I think the girls are better looking, vicious, cool
And the men are flying kites and newsprint
Gets on my arms. I enter rooms –
Wild my steps like an automaton's –
Where batons are linked into some residu.
A gull is eating some garbage.
The sky is an old tomato-can, I think.
I buy a newspaper and begin to walk back.
Smells torture the kites like gulls. Wild gulls, and
It's the tremendous sky of survival.

Few things are still visible to me. Baseball
Withholds the tremors. They fall, so
I drag you down and
You are akimbo as I stick it in
And everything is thunderous accordion April, great,
Risen from palms and hypnotism. I run home
And dip my coffee in bread, and eat some of it.

## You (III)

Today I get this letter from you and the sun
buckles      a mist falls over our villas
with a hideous organic slush like the music of Lawrence Welk
I lay in bed all day, asleep, and like some nocturnal
beast. And get your salutation among the torn green numbers
in the sky over the council houses. And see your eyes when
                         the retired pensioners pass
me by the abandoned railway station – this is not nothing, it is
                         not the hymn
of an age of bankrobbers or heraldic days but it is to sing
with complete gaiety until your heart freaks. I love you.
                         And go down amid the sycamore
summer. Wandering by the lake any way
                         seems lovely, grand, the moon
is a gland in the thigh. Tumble and twinkle as on the golf
                         course apparel
lifts. And a door is opened to
an owl. It is snowing, and you are here on the bed with me
and it is raining, and I am as full of frets as a guitar or a curtain
and I am singing, as I sponge up the cat place. You
                         are heaped
the word reminds me of Abydos and spinach. A curtain
of belief keeps me away from the tombs
of imagery. I love you, I'd like to go.

## You (*IV*)

the chords knotted together like insane nouns        Dante
you are in bed        in the dark copula you
of the musical phrase        a few star birds sing in the branches
their voices are tangled not high
now all of them are dark and some move        you
were a word, in the wood of my life
where the leaves are words, some of them fucking
in obscurity their clasping is terrible and brusque
pain birds ache thru them        and some
are lighter and seem to suggest less
of death than of a viola da gamba player these
birds sweep past in the forest
of my hands on your chest,        as we move
out on the glowing sea of the tropics on an ice pack,        you,

# GEORGE MELLY

## born 1926

### *Homage to René Magritte*

When Magritte died
    The stones fell to the ground
    The birds divorced their leaves
    The night and day agreed to differ
    The breasts became blind
    The cunt was struck dumb
    The tubas extinguished their flames
    The pipe remembered its role
    The words looked up what they meant in the dictionary
    The clouds turned abstract
    The ham closed its eye for ever
When Magritte died.

When Magritte died
    The toes hid modestly in their shoes
    The mountains no longer envied their eagles
    The apple shrunk to the size of an apple
    Or did the room grow to the size of a room?
    The bowler hat lost its ability to astonish
    The old healer
    Returned from a dip in the sea
    Put on his trousers
        his boots
        his cloak
        his hat
Picked up his stick
        his sack
        his cage of doves (clanging its door to)
And set off on his banal journey

When Magritte died.

# GAVIN EWART

born 1916

## Lifelines

In the rat race he won by a whisker.

Bitching and bitching in the double bed.

She came unexpectedly, while he was standing waiting.

A voice from a jar of vaseline: 'This too is love'.

A girl like a cat sits in the window of The Sizzling Sausage.

In the great cities the ants are actuarians.

The lips of the Muse have the taste of beauty.

In a field of alien corn a girl was reaped.

## Lines

The other day I was loving a sweet little fruitpie-and-cream.

He was flying an Avro Manhattan into a beady-eyed silence.

His little shoes were shining as he stood by the sealions.

Panting, she lifted her skirt in a classical gesture.

The darkness came on like an illness while we were debating.

The albatross yawed to the masthead, Coleridge-fashion.

The seven dwarfs were singing these mystical motifs.

## Wanting Out

They're putting Man-Fix on my hair. And through the window
Comes a naked woman with a big whatnot. Oops! I'm away
To a country where the fantasies can be controlled.
Modestly I want to live, modestly. Where the Herr Baron
Takes an Eiswein from the cellar, cradles it gently
In the tiny frozen hands of an echt Deutsch Mimi.
Where the quiet roebuck surround the hunting lodge,
Where the peasants, if they wanted, could shave with their hats.

Take me down to a Lustschloss in the year 1900,
Give me tea on the lawn of a vicarage garden,
Put me in a punt with all my little girl friends,
Let the dreams grow into the leafy sexbooks.
I want a magnifying glass and a knowledge of Coptic
And a box in the British Museum for the last performance of
  Hamlet.

# TOM RAWORTH

born 1938

### My Face Is My Own, I Thought

morning      he had gone
down to the village     a figure
she still recognized from his walk

nothing
         he had explained
is won by arguing     things are changed
only by power
              and cunning     she still sat
meaning to ask what
did you say    ?     echo in her ears

he might just have finished speaking     so
waiting and
             taking the scissors
began to trim off the baby's fingers

### The Empty Pain-Killer Bottles

bite, and the taste of tongues
slimy. drinking spit
she dribbled.

the photographs and secret letters
have melted my wallet, are growing into me
the centipedes are in my veins, swimming against the tide

would i eat her snot under that warm protection?
sure. and listen without laughing
to her tales of mice in the sleeve of that old dress

cheese from her body packed in sandalwood
a pickled finger she gave me as a keepsake
annabella, such a ridiculous name for a breakfast cereal


## Hot Day at the Races

in the bramble bush shelley slowly eats a lark's heart
we've had quite a bit of rain since you were here last
raw silk goes on soft ground (result of looking in the form book)
two foggy dell seven to two three ran
crouched, the blood drips on his knees
and horses pass
shelley knows where the rails end
did i tell you about the blinkered runners?

shelley is waiting with a cross-bow for his rival, the jockey
all day he's watched the races from his bush
now, with eight and a half furlongs to go
raw silk at least four lengths back disputing third place
he takes aim

and horses pass

his rival, the jockey, soars in the air
and falls.      the lark's beak neatly pierces his eye

## *Collapsible*

behind the calm famous faces knowledge of what crimes?
rain on one window showing the wind's direction

a jackdaw collecting phrases        'it's a chicken!'
nothing lonelier than hearing your own pop in another country

               whose face with bandages was singing
her breath always only half an inch from the corner of my eye

# JAMES TATE

born 1943

### The Pet Deer

The Indian Princess
    in her apricot tea gown
    moves through the courtyard
    teasing the pet deer

as if it were her lover.
    The deer, so small and
    confused, slides on the marble
    as it rises on its hindlegs

toward her, slowly, and with
    a sad, new understanding.
    She does not know what
    the deer dreams or desires.

### The Blue Booby

The blue booby lives
on the bare rocks
of Galapagos
and fears nothing.
It is a simple life:
they live on fish,
and there are few predators.
Also, the males do not
make fools of themselves
chasing after the young
ladies. Rather,
they gather the blue
objects of the world
and construct from them

a nest — an occasional
Gaulois package,
a string of beads,
a piece of cloth from
a sailor's suit. This
replaces the need for
dazzling plumage;
in fact, in the past
fifty million years
the male has grown
considerably duller,
nor can he sing well.
The female, though,
asks little of him —

the blue satisfies her
completely, has
a magical effect
on her. When she returns
from her day of
gossip and shopping,
she sees he has found her
a new shred of blue foil:
for this she rewards him
with her dark body,
the stars turn slowly
in the blue foil beside them
like the eyes of a mild savior.

## Dear Reader

I am trying to pry open your casket
with this burning snowflake.

I'll give up my sleep for you.
This freezing sleet keeps coming down
and I can barely see.

If this trick works we can rub our hands
together, maybe

start a little fire
with our identification papers.
I don't know but I keep working, working

half hating you,
half eaten by the moon.


## Love Making

The land floats by under us –
I am kissing you a long time.
Your mouth is full of glass,
your hands are paraffin.

Fields and lakes and woods are spiraling,
little farm cottages
smothered in the morning cool;
then over the city
and many people at work down there.
They have nothing in common with us,
these workers.

Our breath comes out in boxes.
We watch eggshells slowly falling
on the factory rooftops.
Machines crawl into the hills and melt,
workers immediately sleep.
Grass is sprouting
through their backs.

Our eyes are as dry as paper.
We head out over the sea,
and in an hour or so we are coming down.
Into your closet; you
who are now my enemy, leave me.

# LEE HARWOOD

born 1939

## The Words

Clouds scattered across the sky      all so far away
and then the space between      this strange 'distance'
What does 'normal' mean, after all?      you move
toward the window      lights marking the headland
and the night becomes a milestone      though
I      the fog rolls up the hill from the sea
in waves      the town      *desperate?*
Whichever way we look      though so much at hand
only held back by obsessions
but 'home' is so long ago      don't cry

the light's a very pale blue      then maybe      the next time too
a faint glimmer across the bay      neither moon
nor stars
and your letter making signs      concerning 'understanding'
and 'the magic tortoise'      what then?      or just tiredness

At each alternative      the colours in the sky
gradually changing      until you're lulled into believing
you've seen this before      but not quite
The wood-cut of a lone horseman
riding through a deathly countryside      raped

'You're very brave'      I clean the table-top
and you sat in that chair      two red poppies
in the garden below      at dawn
This apparent clumsiness is far from true

## Soft White

When the sea is as grey as her eyes
On these days for sure      the soft white
mist blown in from the ocean      the town dissolving
It all adds up      her bare shoulders

Nakedness      rolling in from the sea
on winter afternoons      a fine rain
looking down on the sand      & shingle
the waves breaking on the shore      & white

It is impossible to deny what
taken by surprise      then wonder
the many details of her body
to be held first now      then later

In body & mind      the fine rain outside
on winter afternoons      the nakedness
of her bare shoulders      as grey as her eyes
the sea rushing up the beach as white as

The whole outline called 'geography'
meeting at a set of erotic points
lips   shoulders   breasts   stomach
the town dissolves      sex   thighs   legs

Outside      then across her nakedness
it rains in the afternoon      then the wonder
her body so young & firm      dissolves the town
in winter      grey as her eyes

## The Final Painting

The white cloud passed over the land
there is sea always round the land
the sky is blue always above the cloud
the cloud in the blue continues to move
– nothing is limited by the canvas or frame –
the white cloud can be pictured like any
other clouds or like a fist of wool
or a white fur rose
The white cloud passes a shadow across
the landscape and so there is a passing greyness
The grey and the white both envelop
the watcher until he too is drawn into the picture
It is all a journey from a room through a door
down stairs and out into the street
The cloud could possess the house
The watchers have a mutual confidence
with the approaching string of white clouds
It is beyond spoken words what they are
silently mouthing to the sky
There was no mystery in this – only the firm
outline of people in overcoats on a hillside
and the line of clouds above them
The sky is blue The cloud white with touches
of grey – the rest – the landscape below –
can be left to the imagination
The whole painting quietly dissolved itself
into its surrounding clouds

## The 'Utopia'

The table was filled with many objects

The wild tribesmen in the hills,
whose very robes were decorated with designs
of a strangeness & upsetting beauty
that went much further than the richly coloured silks
embroidered there could ever suggest; . . .

There were piles of books, yet each one
was of a different size and binding.
The leathers were so finely dyed. The blues
& purples, contrasting with the deceptive simplicity
of the 'natural' tans.
And this prism & arrangement of colours
cannot be set down – the fresh arrangements
& angles possible can only point through a door
to the word 'infinite' made of white puffy clouds
floating high in a blue summer sky;
this has been written there by a small airplane
that is now returning to its green landing field.

The table is very old & made of fine mahogany
polished by generations of servants.
And through the windows the summer blue skies
& white clouds spelling a puffy word.
And on the table the books & examples
of embroidery of the wild hill tribesmen
& many large & small objects – all of which
could not help but rouse a curiosity.

There are at times people in this room
– some go to the table – things are moved –
but the atmosphere here is always that of quiet & calm
– no one could disturb this.
And though the people are the only real threat,

they are all too well trained and aware
to ever introduce the least clumsiness
or disturbing element into the room.

At times it is hard to believe
what is before one's eyes –
there is no answer to this except the room itself,
& maybe the white clouds seen through the window.

No one in the house was sure of the frontiers
& the beautiful atlas gilded and bound with blue silk
was only of antiquarian interest & quite useless
for the new questions. The whole situation
was like a painting within a painting &
that within another & so on & so on –
until everyone had lost sight of their original landmarks.
The heath melted into the sky on the horizon.
And the questions of definition & contrast
only brought on a series of fruitless searches
& examinations that made everyone irritable & exhausted.

Once the surveyors had abandoned their project
the objects once more took over.
It would be false to deny the sigh of relief
there was when this happened & calm returned.

The bus bumped down the avenue
& ahead were the mountains & the woods
that burst into flower as spring settled.
The plan & the heavy revolver were all quite in keeping
with this, despite the apparent superficial
difference & clash of worlds –
there was really only one world.
It wasn't easy – admittedly – & someone
had to stay behind & . . .
The word in the sky had slowly dissolved
& was now nowhere to be seen.
But instead the sun was flooding the whole room

& everything took on a golden aura
— this meant we were even aware of the
band of horsemen now riding through the forest
that surrounded the valley.

The many details may appear evasive
but the purpose of the total was obvious
& uncompromising

# MARK STRAND

### born 1934

## *The Man in the Tree*

I sat in the cold limbs of a tree.
I wore no clothes and the wind was blowing.
You stood below in a heavy coat,
the coat you are wearing.

And when you opened it, baring your chest,
white moths flew out, and whatever you said
at that moment fell quietly onto the ground,
the ground at your feet.

Snow floated down from the clouds into my ears.
The moths from your coat flew into the snow.
And the wind as it moved under my arms, under my chin,
whined like a child.

I shall never know why
our lives took a turn for the worse, nor will you.
Clouds sank into my arms and my arms rose.
They are rising now.

I sway in the white air of winter
and the starling's cry lies down on my skin.
A field of ferns covers my glasses; I wipe them away
in order to see you.

I turn and the tree turns with me.
Things are not only themselves in this light.
You close your eyes and your coat
falls from your shoulders,

the tree withdraws like a hand,
the wind fits into my breath, yet nothing is certain.
The poem that has stolen these words from my mouth
may not be this poem.

## *The Man in Black*

I was walking downtown
when I noticed a man in black,
black cape and black boots, coming toward me.

His arms out in front of him,
his fingers twinkling with little rings,
he looked like a summer night full of stars.

It was summer. The night was full of stars.
The tall buildings formed a hallway down which I walked.
The man in black came toward me.

The waxed tips of his mustache shone
like tiny spears and his teeth glistened.
I offered him my hand which he did not take.

I felt like a fool and stood in his black wake,
shaken and small, and my tears
swung back and forth in the sultry air like chandeliers.

## *The Marriage*

The wind comes from opposite poles,
traveling slowly.

She turns in the deep air.
He walks in the clouds.

She readies herself,
shakes out her hair,

makes up her eyes,
smiles.

The sun warms her teeth,
the tip of her tongue moistens them.

He brushes the dust from his suit
and straightens his tie.

He smokes.
Soon they will meet.

The wind carries them closer.
They wave.

Closer, closer.
They embrace.

She is making a bed.
He is pulling off his pants.

They marry
and have a child.

The wind carries them off
in different directions.

The wind is strong, he thinks
as he straightens his tie.

I like this wind, she says
as she puts on her dress.

The wind unfolds.
The wind is everything to them.

## The Prediction

That night the moon drifted over the pond,
turning the water to milk, and under
the boughs of the trees, the blue trees,
a young woman walked, and for an instant

the future came to her:
rain falling on her husband's grave, rain falling
on the lawns of her children, her own mouth
filling with cold air, strangers moving into her house,

a man in her room writing a poem, the moon drifting into it,
a woman strolling under its trees, thinking of death,
thinking of him thinking of her, and the wind rising
and taking the moon and leaving the paper dark.

# ROBIN MAGOWAN

born 1936

## Zeimbekiko

An old man gets up    turns
As in the quiet darkness of his own empty
Hen scuttled field
He is breaking it
Field goats family stone-cropped house
Takes steps on makes with his hands his white
Fuse of a cigarette crackle sing
In the ash of his glass dancing
His past round whiteness over which he stops
Hops twice          jumps
A needle of browns
Blacks
Occasionally lizard
Flash of a whip salt bright
Falling.

## Zeimbekiko

Says it. His is
Hisses. He takes something round, hard
Word whose shape is a PALM
And smashes it: hands trousers white of nail
Floor darkness with which he scoops slices spins. Is
All things. Mostly is. IS. Is manna is hands is sunwhip
Is the man who says NO I'M NOT old  COOCOOCOOROO
He who brings the red hen out of the grass
Who suncaps shoes & washes the stones
In the verminous oxides of night
And stands there now tongue of crow pieblack hands waiting
He shouts *I hands rain come*
*I am a loaf white*
*I sandpaper grass*

*Looking for you Daddy*
*Who gave me this name of Worm*
*It is the beak of a lemon which spits*
*And unbuttons the splitting greens*
*Of the night where I walk my wound*
*Whose shape is a rooster in my long shipsize arms*
*And the apples of moonlight glow*
A giant fist
Comes out of the mouth dances happy air sings
And a forest of glasses descends
Blinking, in – out, above – below,
Shoes plates hair glittering phosphorescent shirts
Through which he, mosquito bright, glides
White      dipping
Moving over all the floor

moving
threshing
sowing

## Days of 1956

### I

I walk behind you, hand
gripping a stone
I haven't asked you yet
Your sadness
is terrifying, a bird
whose wing
is hurt, & whom I can't
don't know how to, hold
    What do I do: leave
    it there? tell
    someone else?

Over us stars shine, very near, web-footed
as if contained in the spray
We stare out into the shattered gums of the surf
I put out my hands
You take them cup them in yours
Around us
waves splash like broken eggs
which, receding, take on
a mask of molten
grayish-brown
to subside in ashes and silence.


## II

In the sand you compose yourself

the cheek-bones high like the moon
on certain October nights

a funny nose, turned up
at the end

rainy grey-blue eyes

the width appearing again in the hips
which shine like plates
that I take and draw down
into my silence like sky
at the outer edge which as it descends
imposes itself in white
shattering lakes

a sunlight of stones and broken arrows
through which you wade
shoulders hunched
with the uncertainty
of a large heron ready at the first
touch to spring into bluest air.

## Susan

The angelical whites of your eyes
      Of your long
Moon dreaming hands, of your breath
Which when it isn't salt wants roses
      To come and
      Settle there
On the blank sheath of your skin
      Where each pore
Opens & closes itself & becomes fence
      Skirt, meadow
And the colors of all Susan
      All fish, all
      Bright ladders
In the sun of your white & laughing face

## Paros

Paros. A day mild as morning's milk.
Across the bay, beyond where the sea,
A giant crab, pincers in, mountains
Rise immense beneath their morning crust
Of shadow. Higher, having ascended
Through Paros' labyrinth of coiling
Chalk-white streets, cradles to the mouthing wind,
The road spins, high like a waist, its way
Threaded through transparencies of sea-
Whitened olives. Fields ripple out in tiers
Of green and gold speckled with poppies —
As many poppies as green stalks of wheat —
With maybe in a corner the white cube
Of a farmhouse, absolutely modest,
Yet binding fields and sea in the same
Flowing salve of sky.

Ahead the road
Glimmers like a sword, the eye sheering
Downwards past little blue-domed houses
All terrace (with steps like lumps of sugar),
To where in a pot of flame the sea
Funnels the last oils of day, the houses
Reaching their whites down to it like tongues
And up, over an immense distance
Of cobbles, the fresh lime of the stones
Drawing it, skywards, like a first breath
Promise of infinite accession
And happiness.

The sea this Easter
Like soft smoke is everywhere, in the eyes
Of the fishermen who are content
To sit before huge glasses of water
And simply stare, in Prostirakis' voice
Singing with the sea in the pebbles
Of his mouth, the sound high, honeylike,
Reaching over the bay with that flat
Even insistency of serpents
Over grass, until some fisherman
Gets up from his table, hissing, his arm
A mast moving in a white vortex
Over the floor, eyes down, the slow circles
Descending, searching, the sea with him
Naming her, the sound a thread downwards
Through the spool of hisses guiding him as
He steers over its tilting sun-dialed frame
And light pours in swords into him, melting
The streets into a wax, while the head, dis-
Membered, floats out over the singing stones.

# JOHN HAINES

born 1924

## *Awakening*

Soundlessly, a tide at the ear
of the sleeper, a wave
is breaking on an inner shore.

Barriers crumble in the chest,
the arteries surge full and subside,
and flood again ...

And behind the eyelids, a sun
struggling to rise,
throwing its light far inland

where a man neither living nor dying
shifts in his soiled flesh
and remembers ...

## *The Snowbound City*

I believe in this stalled magnificence,
this churning chaos of traffic,
a beast with broken spine,
its hoarse voice hooded in feathers
and mist; the baffled eyes
wink amber and slowly darken.

Of men and women suddenly walking,
stumbling with little sleighs
in search of Tibetan houses –
dust from a far-off mountain
already whitens their shoulders.

When evening falls in blurred heaps,
a man losing his way among churches
and schoolyards feels under his cold hand
the stone thoughts of that city,

impassible to all but a few children
who went on into the hidden life
of caves and winter fires,
their faces glowing with disaster.

### The Flight

It may happen again — this much
I can always believe
when our dawn fills with frightened neighbors
and the ancient car refuses to start.

The gunfire of locks and shutters
echoes next door to the house
left open
for the troops that are certain to come.

We shall leave behind nothing but cemeteries,

and our life like a refugee cart
overturned in the road,
a wheel slowly spinning . . .

### The Cloud Factory

Mountains and cold places on the earth
are no man's garden;
there they make strange uses of rain.

Mist forms in the darkness among peaks
and valleys, like milk beaten thin.

It is rolled into bales,
shot full of damp stars
and pitched down the paths of glaciers.

The dawn wind carries these clouds
into cities and harbors,
to the sick bays and hospitals below.

And all this happens in an air of wrapped
sounds, the silence of bandages.

A magpie is watchman of the cloudworks;
he flies up and down,
the black and white holes of his plumage
disappearing into one another . . .

These are his wounds,
made whole in a cloud of grey feathers.


### A Poem Like a Grenade

It is made to be rolled down
a flight of stairs,
placed under a guilty hat,
or casually dropped into a basket
among the desks
of the wrongheaded statesmen.

As it tumbles on the carpeted stairs
or settles quietly
in its wire-wicker nest,
it begins to unfold,
a ragged flower whose raw petals
burn and scar . . .

Its wastepaper soil catches fire,
the hat is blown from its hook.
Five or six faces are suddenly,
permanently changed . . .

There will be many poems written
in the shape of a grenade –
one hard piece of metal flying off
might even topple a government.

# JOHN DIGBY

born 1938


## Sooner or Later

All my neckties
having been happily strangled
by the sweat of the sun
now froth wildly with loud hosannas
like pickled chilblains

sooner or later
they will glove their mouths
with the fangs of the rain running to China
and turn to face the hands of the south
absolutely black with the smiles of lovers

while they hurry along in my pockets
they stand to attention
to polish a virgin's eyes
cupped between her legs
dancing among the tussocks of yesterday

ah my neckties
swan songs of hideous crows
they cycle furiously back to their birth
in the teeth of the sun
barking like unlaid eggs

soon they will dance again
among the clouds with the thunder
and rinse their hair with sunlight
hanging from the lips of the lightning

## One Night Away from Day

The Army returned home wet with sunlight
Isn't Kent the tyrannosaurus county
Where I shall cut off my head and eat it?
The Doctor muttered to himself
How strange and examined the girl again
Climbing into her bed between
The sheets of frozen fog
She had nests of pipistrelle bats
Sleeping under her pillow
A rather elderly gentleman
That's what he called himself
Suddenly walked into the bedroom
And astonished her by removing his heart
Winding it up and wearing it
As a rather natty wrist-watch
Her father was attempting to stand
On one finger in a glass of water
Someone came along and sprayed
The corpse with ink to stop it smelling
But the damn thing barked all night in her bed
As the lovers strolled through the woods
They happened to glance up among the branches
And saw a herd of cows laying eggs
Usually two to four rarely five or more
A few brave people gathered among the trees
But gradually became frightened
Believing them to be agents of the C.I.A.
They reported the matter to the local police
Who chuckled slyly and said 'watch us'
And with that remark they majestically
Floated up to the ceiling
While the crowd cowered
In sheer terror beneath them

# ANDREI CODRESCU

## born 1946

### *poetry paper*

the great poets are not in the language but in business
because what poet can make cut production costs equal
infinite compassion, offhand, in a matter of fact way
and in a tone that excludes misunderstanding? not only
do the great poets now sit outside language manipulating
the heart but also the great readers of poetry who,
stunned in the past by the printed page, are now free
to have dinner and board a bus in the company of sheer
poetry with not a thought for their own failings which,
quite apart from their bodies, they now take to the
doctors to get fixed? in our time, we elevate details
to the power of numbers, to the place where concrete
representation has flown the coop, and one day we will
see ourselves translated in machinery and this, thank
god, will be the day when i will unscrew my head with
the silence of my surroundings and go to sleep forever.

### *a grammar*

i was dead and i wanted peace
then i was peaceful and not quite dead yet
then i was in my clothes
and i took them off and then
there was too much light
and night fell
then i wanted to talk to somebody
and i spoke ecstatically
and i was answered on time in every language
in a beautiful way
but i felt unloved and everyone
came to love me

still there is something running
and i can't catch it
i am always behind


### the imagination of necessity

there comes a time when everything is laced
the water you drink      the words you speak
your manner of turning      of being
& the substance
is undefinable      coloratura of a
scale moving backwards into embryo tonality
which is not so bad when you possess a technique
of encounter or a professional philosophy
when you are a baker or an expert
lover      which is terrible when you live
with a rope around your neck a flower in your cock
a windlike disability      a flight pattern
drawn in the wrong sky in the wrong season
ducks sucked out of migration into disarray
oh concentrate then!      if you can
on the mystery ingredient      imagine your body
a spoon stirring the sugar at the bottom of a vast
cup of tea & the melting strings of sugar
on which the angels of hot water
climb with ferocious aptitude      what this imagining
gives      besides a headache      is an ease
of penetration a fluidity in entering strange
houses      a lack of weight in taking what's not yours
but fits you      & good luck

## work

at night the day is constantly woken up
by exploding dream objects
until all our days are tired
and collapse on our hearts like loud
zippers breaking in the middle.
i sleep in the daytime with my head on the piano.
i sleep at night too standing on the roof.
i sleep all the sleep that is given me plus
the sleep of those who can't sleep and the sleep
of great animals who lie wounded
and unable to sleep.
i'm dead tired from the work everyone does
ceaselessly around me, from the work the morning
crowds are going to do after they are thrown up
by the thousand mouths of toast and cologne
into the buses and subways,
from the work the plants do to get water
from the labors of beasts looking for meat
from the labors of speaking replying writing
from the work going on inside me with a million
greedy cells beating the shit out of each other
from the work of the sun turning around
and the earth turning around it.
i'm tired in general and sleepy in particular.
i have a great desire to move elsewhere.

# W. S. MERWIN

born 1927

### *Bread*

*for Wendell Berry*

Each face in the street is a slice of bread
wandering on
searching

somewhere in the light the true hunger
appears to be passing them by
they clutch

have they forgotten the pale caves
they dreamed of hiding in
their own caves
full of the waiting of their footprints
hung with the hollow marks of their groping
full of their sleep and their hiding

have they forgotten the ragged tunnels
they dreamed of following in out of the light
to hear step after step
the heart of bread
to be sustained by its dark breath
and emerge

to find themselves alone
before a wheat field
raising its radiance to the moon

## A Door

You walk on

carrying on your shoulders
a glass door
to some house that's not been found

there's no handle

you can't insure it
can't put it down

and you pray please let me not
fall please please let
me not drop
it

because you'd drown like water
in the pieces

so you walk on with your hands frozen
to your glass wings
in the wind
while down the door in time with your feet
skies are marching
like water down the inside of a bell

those skies are looking for you
they've left everything
they want you to remember them

they want to write some last phrase
on you
you

but they keep washing off
they need your ears
you can't hear them

they need your eyes
but you can't look up
now

they need your feet oh
they need your feet
to go on

they send out their dark birds for you
each one the last
like shadows of doors calling calling
sailing
the other way

so it sounds like good-bye

### *To the Hand*

What the eye sees is a dream of sight
what it wakes to
is a dream of sight

and in the dream
for every real lock
there is only one real key
and it's in some other dream
now invisible

it's the key to the one real door
it opens the water and the sky both at once
it's already in the downward river
with my hand on it
my real hand

and I am saying to the hand
turn

open the river


## Glass

One day you look at the mirror and it's open
and inside the place where the eyes were
is a long road gray as water
and on it someone is running away
a little figure in a long pale coat
and you can't move you can't call
it's too late for that
who was it you ask

then there are many of them
with their backs to you and their arms in the air
and no shadows
running away on the road gray as ice
with the leaves flying after them
and the birds in great flocks the dust
the stones the trees
all your terrors running away from you
too late
into a cloud

and you fall on your knees and try to call to them
far in the empty face

## The Diggers

If a man with a shovel came down the road

if two men
with shovels came down the road
if eight men with shovels
came down the road

if seventeen men with shovels came down the road
and I wanted to hide
I would see then that everything here
is transparent

yes that is what I would see but I would feel myself
then like my hand in front of my eyes
like this hand just as it is
in front of my eyes

and I would try to take it down
before they saw through it and found me

# BERT MEYERS

born 1928

## Pigeons

Wherever I go to find
peace or an island
under palms in the afternoon
at midnight to pity my neighborhood
at dawn in the shrubs
to look for a child

I hear them
they fly by
applauding themselves
I see them
they pray as they walk
their eyes are halos
around a pit
they look amazed

Who are these that come
as a cloud to our windows
who rush up like smoke
before the town burns

You will find one
on a mountain
in a carpenter's shop
at home on the lawn
of an old estate
at the library
in the forehead of paradise

Whoever is mad
can accuse them
thousands were killed in a day

What happens to them
happens to me
when I can't sleep
they moan and I'm there
and it's still like that

## Suburban Dusk

One girl in a red dress leaves the shopping center with empty hands: and you believe in the future – you've seen a drop of blood flee from the luminous cells of a corpse.

But the sky slips a coin in the slot between two buildings. Lights go on. Distorted creatures appear. A car, like an angry heart, explodes.

And a vast erysipelas spreads over the hills. What can you do? Each night, the city becomes a butterfly, trembling in its oil.

## Daybreak

Birds drip from the trees.
The moon's a little goat
over there on the hill;
dawn, as blue as her milk,
fills the sky's tin pail.

The air's so cold a gas station
glitters in an ice-cube.
The freeway hums like a pipe
when the water's on.
Streetlights turn off their dew.

The sun climbs down from a roof,
stops by a house and strikes
its long match on a wall,
takes out a ring of brass keys
and opens every door.

# MICHAEL McCLURE

born 1932

## Rant Block

THERE IS NO FORM BUT SHAPE! NO LOGIC BUT
[SEQUENCE!
SHAPE the cloak and being of love, desire, hatred,
hunger. BULK or BODY OF WHAT WE ARE AND
[STRIVE
FOR. ((OR
there is a series of synaptic
stars. Lines of them. It's that simple
or brutal. And, worst, they
become blurred.

SNOUT EYES
As negative as beauty is.))
LEVIATHAN WE SWOOP DOWN AND COVER
what is ours. Desires
OR BLOCK THEM. SICKNESS – ACHES.
Are heroes in simplicity with open eyes
and hungers. Truth
does not hurt us. Is more difficult than
beauty is. We smolder smoke pours
from our ears in stopping what we feel.
(free air)
Your hand, by your side, is never love.

FORM IS AN EVASION! POETRY
A PATTERN TO BE FILLED BY FAGGOTS.

WILD ANGER MORE THAN CULTIVATED LOVE!!
Wolf and salmon shapes free to kill
for food love and hatred.
Life twists its head *from side to side* to test
the elements and seek
for breath and meat to feed on.

# I AM A FIRE AND I MOVE IN AN INFERNO
sick I smolder
and do not burn clear.
Smoldering makes nets of smoke upon the world.
I am clean free and radiant and beauty follows this.
Not first but follows.
What is love or hatred but a voice I hear
of what I see and touch. Who is the man
within that moves me that I never see
but hear and speak to? Who are you
to stop me? Why are you here
to block me? All I choose to see
is beauty. Nerves. Inferno!
Fakery of emotions. Desire for presumption. Love of glory. Pride.
Vanity. Dead and unfilled desires. Regrets. Tired arms. Tables. Lies.
BLOOD AND MUSCLE BLOOD AND MUSCLE
[BLOOD AND MUSCLE BLOOD AND MUSCLE
Calling pure love lust to block myself and die with that upon my
[head?
Wit and false stupidity with no point to it but the most tangled ends
unwitnessed by myself in fulfillment. When I found you sleeping
why didn't I? Would you love me for it? Do I care? OH. And
[smoke.

AND NOT THAT FINE SWING
of wing or fin!


And never chivalry. The strive to rise. The act of grace. Of self.
Of sureness large enough for generosity. The overflowing.
But the chiding carping voice and action. What is this? Why
DONT WE KICK IN THE WALLS? KICK IN THE
[WALLS!
INVENT OURSELVES IN IMAGES OF WHAT WE
[FEEL.

WHERE HAVE ALL THESE CLOUDS OF SMOKE
[COME FROM?

I am the animal seraph that I know I am!

And I burn with fine pure love and fire, electricity and oxygen
a thing of protein and desire,  !!
and all of this is ugliness and talk not freedom
OH SHIT HELL FUCK THAT WE ARE BLOCKED
in striving by what we hate
surrounding us. And do not break it in our strike
at it. The part of us
so trained to live in filth and never stir.
THAT I WAIT FOR YOU TO RAISE YOUR HAND
[FIRST

(to me)
This is sickness. This is what
I hate within
myself. This
is the war I battle in. This is the neverending instant.
The black hour that never ceases. This is the darkness about
the burning.
The form and talk of form as if flames obeyed without
dwindling.

These are the dull words from an animal of real flesh. Why?
Where is the fire in them?
Never let them stop until they are
moving things. Until
they stir the fire!
Never let them stand stemmed by form again. Let
my face be radiant and give off light!
Never allow sign of love where hatred dwells!

If there are bastions, let my love be walls!

## Moiré

*for Francis Crick*

1. THE CHANTING IN TIBET HAS NOT CEASED –
   IT IS AS IMMORTAL AS MEAT.
2. HORNS, CYMBALS, AND LIGHTNING BOLTS
   OVER GLACIERS.
3. BEARDED SEA OTTERS CRACKING MUSSELS
   ON STONES ON THEIR STOMACHS.
4. COYOTES LAUGH AND PRANCE ON POINT
   REYES.
5. REVIVE THE PLEISTOCENE.
6. PLEISTOCENE IS NOT GLACIO-THERMAL –
   IT IS MEAT-MAMMALIAN.
7. CRACKS IN THE SIDEWALK REFLECT THE
   DISPERSION OF CLOUDS AND AURAS OF
   COLOR.
8. REALITY IS A POINT, A PLATEAU, A MYSTERY.
9. IT MAY BE PENETRATED.
10. WILDFLOWERS: MAN ROOT, SEPTEMBER
    BLACKBERRIES, MONKEYFLOWERS.
11. POEMS AND PERCEPTIONS PENETRATE THE
    PLATEAU.
12. SUCCULENT GARDENS HANG ON CLIFFS.
13. THE VELVET BUTTERFLY AND THE SMILING
    WEASEL.
14. BENIGN VISAGES FLOATING IN AIR.
15. SPIRIT IS ACTION.
16. ACTION IS PROTEIN.
17. BONES OF THE SABER TUSK IN ASPHALT.
18. MOTILE POEMS LIKE FINGERS OR ROOT
    TIPS.
19. AMINO TRIGGERS IN SPACE.
20. WE ARE ACTIVITY.
21. BELOW US IS STEADY AND SOLID.
22. SOON ENOUGH.

23. PERHAPS WE RETURN TO A POOL – STEADY AND SOLID.
24. NO MATTER – ANTI-MATTER.
25. WE HAVE THE JOY OF HERETICS.
26. WE DID NOT CHOOSE IT – WE ARE.
27. PERFECT.
28. PERFECT PLATEAU BECOMING ODORS AND TOUCHES.
29. I DID NOT KNOW THIS IS NATURE.
30. THE BLANKET FLOWS OUT OF THE WINDOW – ON IT ARE YELLOW BANDS WOVEN WITH RED BISON.
31. SOLID BLACKNESS ABOVE AND BELOW.
32. MUSIC BETWEEN.
33. FORESTS OF MOSS IN THE COLD STREAM.
34. BULK OF A DEAD SEA LION – DARK EYES OPEN.
35. THE DESERT IS ALIVE.
36. THE FIR FEELS THE SOLSTICE.
37. SENSE HORIZONTALLY, ASPIRE VERTI-CALLY – *AGNOSIA*.
38. KEATS, DIRAC, DIONYSIUS THE AREOPA-GITE.
39. TRUMPETS, CYMBALS, WARM GRASS, ROAR OF A MOTORCYCLE.
40. LEATHER, QUARTZ, AND CINNAMON.
41. DISSOLUTION IS A PRIVILEGE.
42. HAIL PLANARIAN!
43. SWEET, WARM AND ODOROUS IN THE AUTUMN SUN.
44. BLACKER THAN BLACK, BLUE-BLACK – A MIRROR REFLECTING REDS.
45. SCREAMS AND FLAMES OVER THE HORIZON.
46. CREAK OF EUCALYPTUS BOUGHS.
47. THE PLATEAU IS A POINT, THE MASK OF A DIMENSION.
48. THE MASK IS ENFORCED BY ENSOCIALIZA-TION OF PERCEPTIONS.

49. SEPTEMBER BLACKBERRIES ARE FREE.
50. THERE ARE STILL BLOSSOMS.
51. CONDENSATION FALLS PATTERING ON LEAVES.
52. MACHINE GUNS COMMUNICATE BULLETS.
53. BOMBS ARE SYMBOLS FOR MEAT THOUGHTS.
54. FACES OF MALEVOLENCE AND FOLLY STARE FROM THE WALLS.
55. THE FLEECE MOVING IN THE BREEZE BY THE FIRE IS LOVELY.
56. WE ARE OLD WOLVES, INDIANS, CREATURES.
57. ETERNITY BECOMES BROWN-GOLD FOR AN INSTANT.
58. TIME IS THE LONG WAY BACK.
59. IGNORANCE, LIKE INFORMATION, IS A LEVER.
60. THE BODY'S ODORS – THE BERRY'S ODORS.
61. THE MASS OF INFORMATION WHITES OUT.
62. RAINBOW AGAINST WHITE – PROJECTED ON BLACK.
63. THE SELVES FLYING THROUGH THE BODY HAVE FACES.
64. THEY STREAM WITH TAILS OF COLORS.
65. SENSATION MAY PRECEDE INFORMATION.
66. WE DIVE BOTH DOWN AND OUTWARD.
67. SOLIDITY AND VIBRATION.
68. UNEXPECTED PROFILES AND FACES.
69. THE BRAMBLE TANGLE IS A MOVING SCULPTURE.
70. DRAGONS OF SPACE AND MATTER.
71. FALSE PERCEPTIONS MIMIC THE REAL – A COVER.
72. THE BODY MAY BE DIAGRAMMED WITH COLORS AND ODORS.
73. THERE IS A FIRE AND TRAJECTORIES OF ENERGIES.
74. BEYOND THE MASK OF THE POINT ARE

TRILLIONIC INTERLOCKED CONSTELLA-
TIONS.

75. PLEASURES ARE NOT RELATIVE BUT
ACTUAL – BLACKBERRIES, SEA LIONS,
TENDRILS.

76. PERCEPTIONS ARE HERETIC – THEY
NEGATE ABSENCE.

77. ABSENCE IS LACK OF PERCEPTION.

78. THE MUSSEL SHELL CRACKS ON THE ROCK.

79. WAVES OF WATER AND PROTOPLASM.

80. COYOTE SHIT – THE TAJ MAHAL.

81. WINGED TIGERS ENCASED IN TRANS-
PARENT SILVER.

82. MY WHISKERS – THE WOLF'S BEARD.


*From the Window of the Beverly Wilshire Hotel*

THE WOLF'S PROFILE HANGS
OVER THE THREE CROSSES
and is engraved with the letters
of the alphabet.
His eye is an Italian movie.
Drops of blood
flow from the trees.
It is all carved on an onyx
and laid on the grass
surrounded by fluttering flags.

---

The entire structure
stands on a papier-mâché pedestal
that is cleverly gilded
and antiqued. Its eagle claw
feet are strapped
with black leather

and silver buckles
to the back of a trained turtle
who swims in white steaming chowder
in which float pieces of rainbows,
shards of gold leaf,
and cases of green eye liner.


*May Morn*

TUNING MYSELF BY MORNING COFFEE
– the cup makes steam in the shapes
of goddesses. Molecules
swirl in air. California
edges into sun. Waves lash against
Point Bonita. I sit
– the last Indian –
beating on my drum.
My tee shirt the color
of raspberries – blazoned
with yellow planets.
I am as mad (or sane)
as Shelley
waiting
to be a magian
– resting for action.
AH,
there are doors of tissue gold . . .

*Postscript*

# ANNE WALDMAN and TED BERRIGAN

born 1945                              born 1934

Selections from *Memorial Day: a collaboration*

& Now the book is closed
The windows are closed                 The door is closed
        The house is closed

                                The bars are closed

The gas station is closed

                                The streets are closed
                The store is closed
        The car is closed

                        The rain is closed
                Red is closed
                & yellow is closed
                & green is closed

The bedroom is closed

                        The desk is closed
                                The chair is closed

                The geraniums are closed
                        The triangle is closed
                                The orange is closed
        The shine is closed         The sheen is closed
                The light is closed

The cigar is closed

                        The dime is closed
                The pepsi is closed
The airport is closed

                        The mailbox is closed
                The fingernail is closed


        The ankle is closed

                                The skeleton is closed
                The melon is closed
        The angel is closed          The football is closed
        The coffee is closed          The grass is closed

The tree is closed
The sky is dark
The dark is closed
The bridge is closed
The movie is closed
The girl is closed          The gods are closed
The blue is closed
The white is closed
The sun is closed
The ship is closed
The army is closed
The war is closed
The poolcue is closed
Six is closed
eight is closed
four is closed
Seven is closed
The lab is closed          The bank is closed          The Times is closed
The leaf is closed
The bear is closed
Lunch is closed
New York City is closed
Texas is closed
New Orleans is closed

Miami is closed
Okmulgee is closed
Sasebo is closed
Cranston is closed
The Fenway is closed
Bellevue is closed
Columbia is closed
9th Street is closed
2nd Street is closed
First Avenue is closed
Horatio St is closed
66 is closed
Painting is closed          Leibling is closed

Long Island is closed
Stones are closed          The afternoon is closed
The friends are closed
          & Daddy is closed
               & brother is closed & sister is closed
Your mother is closed
          & I am closed – & I am closed
               & tears are closed
& the hole is closed    & the boat has left    & the day is closed.

1971

# Index of First Lines

A selection of books published by Penguin is listed on the following pages.

For a complete list of books available from Penguin in the United States, write to Dept. DG, Penguin Books, 299 Murray Hill Parkway, East Rutherford, New Jersey 07073.

For a complete list of books available from Penguin in Canada, write to Penguin Books Canada Limited, 2801 John Street, Markham, Ontario L3R 1B4.

If you live in the British Isles, write to Dept. EP, Penguin Books Ltd, Harmondsworth, Middlesex.

*Peter and Linda Murray*

## A DICTIONARY OF ART AND ARTISTS
### Fourth Edition

This dictionary covers the last seven centuries, up to Pablo Picasso and Pop Art. Short biographies of nearly a thousand painters, sculptors, and engravers fill the greater part of it; these contain facts and dates of the artist's career, a note of galleries exhibiting his work, and an estimate of his style. The dictionary also defines artistic movements, terms applied to periods and ideas, and technical expressions and processes. The art of Eastern or primitive peoples is not covered. 'A vast amount of information intelligently presented, carefully detailed, abreast of current thought and scholarship and easy to read' – *The Times Literary Supplement* (London). 'A thorough, well-documented . . . and at the same time imaginative opus' – Dr. J. P. Hodin, *College Art Journal*.